MW00440179

A TIME TO FORGIVE

KAY CORRELL

ROSE QUARTZ PRESS

Published by Rose Quartz Press

041119

This book is dedicated to my husband and sons. For their unwavering support. For the spontaneous parties they throw to celebrate my successes. For being by my side during the tough times. I'm the luckiest wife and mother in the world. I love you all so much.

Let's go singing in the rain…

KAY'S BOOKS

Find more information on all my books at
kaycorrell.com

COMFORT CROSSING ~ THE SERIES

Lighthouse Point series - with Josephine and
Paul from The Letter.)

LIGHTHOUSE POINT ~ THE SERIES
Wish Upon a Shell - Book One
Wedding on the Beach - Book Two
Love at the Lighthouse - Book Three
Cottage near the Point - Book Four
Return to the Island - Book Five
Bungalow by the Bay - Book Six

SWEET RIVER ~ THE SERIES
A Dream to Believe in - Book One
A Memory to Cherish - Book Two
A Song to Remember - Book Three
A Time to Forgive - Book Four
A Summer of Secrets - Book Five

INDIGO BAY ~ A multi-author sweet romance series
Sweet Sunrise - Book Three
Sweet Holiday Memories - A short holiday story
Sweet Starlight - Book Nine

Sign up for my newsletter at my website
kaycorrell.com to make sure you don't miss any
new releases or sales.

CHAPTER 1

Bree Stuart paused with her hand on the worn door handle to her parents' cabin on Lone Elk Lake. Her hand trembled slightly, and her pulse thrummed through her veins. Twenty years since she'd walked through this door. She briefly considered turning around, jumping into her car, and driving back to Austin to her safe little house. Though when she reminded herself the drive had taken over fifteen hours, she wasn't that anxious to leap back on the road.

She quickly realized she hadn't grabbed the cabin key from her car—of course, that hadn't been on purpose—and crossed back to her ten-year-old functional red sedan to snatch the key out of the console between the seats. It had taken her forever to find the stupid key back at her home. She'd finally found it stashed in the bottom of her jewelry box, in an envelope with a silver bracelet and deliberately forgotten memories.

Bree closed the car door and glanced at the faded sign by the front door of the cabin. Stuart Chateau, a particularly grandiose name for a quiet lake cabin. The small wooden sign had hung by the front door for over thirty years. She ran her fingers across the faded lettering, and bittersweet memories bubbled up and threatened to rise to the surface. Something she just couldn't allow.

She crossed to the front door, momentarily praying her parents had changed the locks so she would have an excuse to turn around and drive home. No such luck. The key turned easily in the lock, and the door jerked open with her not-so-gentle push, almost causing her to tumble into the cabin. Her heart beat a double-time rhythm, and she drew in a deep breath of courage. She stepped over the threshold and had to grab ahold of the doorway to steady herself.

The cabin looked the same. For some reason, she'd thought it would look different now. It had been twenty years since she'd last crossed that threshold, since she'd walked those floors, looked out the windows at the views. Twenty years since she'd talked and laughed and shared meals with family and friends. She looked around the great room and across to the doors on the far wall with an expansive view of the lake. The old sliding doors had been replaced with French doors. That was new. The entire lakeside of the house opened up to a wide, come-have-a-party deck.

The smell of old furniture and closed-up house mixed in with the familiar smell of... what? She didn't know. But to her, it would always be the cabin scent. She swore she could smell it in her dreams... and her nightmares.

She pushed away the memories and reminded herself why she was here. She'd always been the responsible sister, the one who did what needed to be done. Well, except for the one thing her parents had always wanted from her and she'd never been able to give them. She regretted that, but she'd done the best she could. Some things just couldn't be forgotten.

Bree looked around the cabin, trying to convince herself to actually step inside. Why was she the one who had to do this? Maybe they could just hire someone to fix up the place to get it ready to sell. Her sisters hadn't even thought about all Bree was doing as the executor of their parents' will. She was the only sister who'd thought to check on the cabin before they put it on the market to see what needed to be done to get it ready. She wasn't sure if her sisters ever went to the lake anymore.

She pushed her shoulders back and determinedly crossed into the depths of the cabin, fighting her urge to run. The kitchen was in the corner of the great room, with a bar-height counter separating it from the rest of the open area of the main level of the cabin. A trio of bar stools with floral cushions nestled under the counter. A loft grazed the top of the vaulted ceiling. Memories flitted around her of the many nights sleeping up there as a child, whispering and giggling with her sisters until their mother insisted they go to sleep. The girls had bedrooms, but many nights, when they were younger, they preferred to sleep up in the loft together. She could almost hear the echoes of muffled voices, threatening to dance alive in her memories, but she flattened them dead.

Bree crossed to the kitchen and dropped her purse on the counter. She noticed, with a smile, her mom had finally replaced the stove top with the two cranky burners that, at any given moment, no one ever knew if they'd work.

She walked over and ran her hand over the worn wooden table in the dining area, tracing the grain of the oak top. Even though it was chilly, she threw open a set of the French doors to the deck to try and get some fresh air into the place.

The cabin was at the end of Lone Elk Lake where it arched around to form a small, peaceful cove. The banks were lined with pine trees and rocks. She stared out at the view, mesmerized. The cool air rushed over her, and she drew in a cleansing breath of the crisp, pine-scented breeze.

She crossed over to the faded floral sofa and dropped down onto it, propping her feet on the old trunk of her grandma's they'd used for a coffee table.

The place felt so like home, and yet so foreign. She'd spent so many of her summers and weekends there as a young girl. Then when she'd gotten to college age, she started working summer jobs in Sweet River Falls, driving down from college at Boulder to live at the summer cabin and work at a variety of summer jobs. She and her sisters, Abby and Cece, had run with the same crowd of friends, summer after summer. Until the year Bree turned twenty and her world had fallen apart.

Well, that was the first time her world had fallen apart. The second time it had crashed was three years ago when her husband left her. He just hadn't wanted to be married to her anymore. Didn't love her. Wanted out. It had turned out what he did want was a woman ten years younger than Bree with pouty lips and long blonde hair. And then a series of young women. There was no changing it now. She drew in a quick breath, fighting off the rising anger.

Then there was this last time her world disintegrated into tiny broken pieces, the one that just about broke her completely. She was still numb from this last one, and it had been almost a year.

And if the universe hadn't been cruel enough to her, six months ago, her parents had died in a car accident. Her heart ached with all the losses in her life, the regrets, and the dashed hopes. She wasn't sure she knew how to feel anymore. Life had taught her to shut down to protect herself. She'd raised shutting off her emotions to an art form.

A breeze drifted in through the open doors —a soothing breeze if she were just able to be soothed these days. Something she'd almost decided would never happen again. She had so much anger and resentment boiling inside, tucked safely away under the pretense of no feelings. No talking to a therapist or any amount of rational thinking had been able to change the fact. She'd turned into a bitter woman she barely recognized and didn't like much these days.

Being at the lake cabin wasn't going to help one tiny little bit. At all. It was just going to smack her in the face with the memory of when her life all started down the slippery slope that led... right back to the lake cabin, she guessed. She let out a long, drawn-out sigh.

She needed to get to work. Still, she just sat and stared out at the cove.

A brisk knock at the door startled her from her reverie. Who could that be? No one even knew she was here. She thought about ignoring it, but it was obvious she was here, with her car parked smack in the middle of the driveway. She pushed up off the couch and went to tug the door open, making a mental note to oil the hinges so it opened without wrenching out her shoulder. She was sure a door that fought back wasn't the best first impression for anyone wanting to buy the cabin.

The door yanked open, and there, filling the doorway with his energy and smile, was Jason Cassidy. Looking older, with the tiniest touch of gray at the temples and scattered through his dark brown hair. His face was weathered now, but the unmistakable sparkle in his chestnut brown eyes was still there.

"Breester!" He swept her up in a no-questions-asked hug, as if sure she would welcome it.

And she did. He wrapped her in acceptance and happiness and the comfortable feeling of an old, cherished quilt. It felt foreign and delicious. Even if she'd deserted him for years, with rare Christmas cards and even rarer phone calls.

Breester. His pet name for her. She'd almost forgotten all about it. He'd given it to her when she'd complained that her sisters both had nicknames. Cecelia was nicknamed Cece, and

Abigail was usually called Abby. But how did one shorten Bree? She still remembered him laughing and telling her he'd lengthen her name to Breester. It sounded so good and welcoming and familiar coming from his rumbling deep voice.

Names and nicknames were funny things. She'd always been slightly annoyed when everyone called the sisters the ABC girls—Abby, Bree, and Cece.

"Jason. You're looking good." She pushed away slightly as he set her back down.

"I drove by and saw the car and thought I'd check and see who was here."

"It's just me."

"I was sorry to hear about your parents. That's really tough, huh?"

"Yes, it is." Her voice was low and suddenly choked with emotions she thought she'd finally been able to shove away. Evidently not.

"You just here to get away for a bit?"

He totally ignored the fact that he knew darn well she hadn't been here in twenty years.

"No, I'm going to get the cabin ready to put on the market."

"No. You girls are selling it?" His eyes

questioned her, asking her more than what he actually voiced.

"Well, I can't afford the cabin and my house in Austin. Cece doesn't have the money for it either, and Abby has no interest in it. So we're going to sell it."

"That's too bad. Kind of an end to an era."

"I guess. One I'm ready to end." She shoved her hair back from her face, the brown curls tumbling rebelliously right back to bug her. "I need to see if I can get it ready to put on the market. Make sure everything is in working order. See if I can touch up the painting and do little stuff that makes it look more inviting."

"Wow. I can't believe you're selling it. It will seem so...*wrong*... having someone else own the place. Guess we'll have to rename it something other than Stuart Chateau, too."

"Yeah, I guess." Her voice choked. Maybe this was going to be harder to part with than she thought.

She read the empathy in his warm brown eyes. He'd always been able to figure her out, usually before she had herself figured out.

"I've missed you, Bree." He reached out and touched her arm.

"I know. I missed you too. I just couldn't..."

"I understand. I had hoped that over time, you'd work it all out and come back." He lounged against the doorframe.

She shook her head. "Some things just can't be forgotten... or forgiven."

"That's too bad. I hoped... Well, never mind. Let's not talk about the past." A grin slanted across his tanned features. "Let's talk about dinner. Tonight. Over at the lodge. My treat."

"Oh, I don't know, Jase."

"Come on, Mom would love to see you. Six o'clock?"

She gave in. She'd never been able to resist his smile. He'd been one of her closest friends for twelve years of her childhood. From the year she turned eight and her parents bought the cabin until the year she turned twenty. His Mom owned Sweet River Lodge just over the hill on the main part of the lake. There had been a worn trail over the hill when she'd been younger. She doubted a pathway even existed anymore.

"Okay, I'll be over at six."

Jason flashed a cocky grin like he'd known he'd win her over. "That's great. I'll tell Mom. She'll be so excited."

"Guess the path is gone and I'll need to drive around, huh?"

"Nope. The path is still there. I keep it trimmed up. I always hoped you girls would come back and use it someday. Besides, the guests at the lodge like to climb to the top of the hill for the view of the lake. We have a gazebo up on top now."

"Okay, I guess I'll walk over there then. Just like old times."

"It will be great to look up and see you coming down the hill again. I've missed that." He gave her another quick hug and crossed over to his truck. "Don't stand me up, Breester."

"I'll be there, I promise." She waved to him while he climbed into his old blue pickup truck and it ground to life. He pulled out of the driveway with a spray of loose gravel and a quick wave of his hand.

"Mom, you here?" Jason walked into his mother's cabin at Sweet River Lodge.

Nora Cassidy came walking out of the laundry room, carrying a basket of neatly folded clothes. "Right here."

"I have a surprise. Guess who's coming to dinner at the lodge tonight?"

His mother smiled and shifted the basket to her hip. "No clue."

"Bree Stuart."

His mother's eyes widened. "Really? We haven't seen her in... well, I don't know how long it's been. Fifteen? Twenty years? Is she back at the cabin?"

"She is." Jason reached for the basket. "Here, I'll put this back in your bedroom."

He returned to find his mother in the kitchen. She held up a mug. "Coffee?"

"I always have time for a quick one." He took the offered mug and a sip of the delicious brew made from locally roasted coffee beans.

"So, she finally came back for a visit, huh?" Nora grabbed a mug of coffee for herself and leaned against the counter.

"Not really. She said they were getting ready to sell the place."

"I'd heard her parents died. So unexpectedly, that's sad. I guess the girls don't want the cabin?"

"I don't think any of them can afford the upkeep on their own and, well, she said it just made sense to sell it."

"Probably get a better price now before news gets out about Dobbs wanting to sell his property and change the zoning laws."

"We won't let that happen." Jason pressed a quick kiss on his mother's cheek. "Even though Beth dropped out of the race for mayor, we still can lobby against the changes."

"Well, some people in the town would like the zoning changed. If more big condo complexes are built out here on the lake, it would mean more tourists in town, more business, more jobs."

"I hope it doesn't come to that." He sighed. The lake was just about the most perfect place on earth as far as he was concerned, and he loved helping his mother run the lodge nestled between the banks of Sweet River and Lone Elk Lake.

"How does Bree look?"

"The same. Well, older. Sadder."

"She's had some tough blows in life. Last time Abby was at the cabin, she came to the lodge for dinner. Said that Bree had gotten divorced."

"I heard that. That's too bad." He took one last gulp of his coffee. "I've got to run. The tractor is acting up and I need it in tiptop shape before any of the big winter storms hit." He set his mug in the sink. "I'll see you tonight at the lodge. I told Bree to come over about six."

"I'll see you then. Looking forwarding to seeing Bree again."

CHAPTER 2

Bree finally coaxed the water heater to spit out some lukewarm—no, maybe luke*cool* water—so she could take a quick shower. A *really* quick shower. She grabbed a towel and dried off in a hurry. Better add look at the water heater to her growing to-do list.

She pulled on a pair of jeans, a warm sweater, and boots. It would be good to see Jason's mom, Nora. The woman had always had a place at the table for any of Jason's friends who might drop by. The lodge's dining hall did a brisk business on the weekends during the summer and a fair business during the weekdays. Nora kept one table in the corner for friends and family who stopped by. Bree could remember many a night she'd pop up from the table and help deliver a meal to a big group of diners, or help clear off a table during the rush and set it up for the next customers.

She hadn't thought about those nights in years. Now she couldn't wait to get over to the lodge. After grabbing her parka and gloves, she tugged the door behind her and yanked it again until she could finally get it to close all the way. She hurried down the gravel drive and crossed the blacktop road. She walked down the road and slightly around the bend. There, heading up the hill, was the pathway, the shortcut to the lodge. More overgrown than when she was a girl, but still there, calling her name. Beckoning her to climb the hill and disappear into her past.

She resolutely put one foot on the pathway and started her ascent. When she got to the top of the hill, she saw the cute white gazebo the Cassidys had built on the crest of the hill. She sank down on a bench and looked out at the view. The lake stretched out before her and the snowcapped mountains rose majestically in the distance. The sun was beginning to set and threw a bouquet of brilliant colors across the sky. She'd missed this view, too. How many times had she and Jason or she and her sisters sat up here talking? Then it had been on an old log, not on a nice bench in a gazebo. She could almost hear their young, girlish voices. But no, it had been forever since the three of them had sat up here. Twenty years was a long time, she reminded herself. A long time—but not long enough.

She rested a moment, taking in the view, feeling the cool breeze, listening to the wind through the trees. She'd loved the lake in the summer on the weekdays. When the crowds were not so overwhelming, but the warm summer days blended one into the next. All three sisters had held a series of part-time jobs with no serious responsibilities. Life had been simple then.

Well, until it had gotten complicated.

She rose and took one last look at the view, then turned and headed down the hillside toward the lodge. Another overwhelming feeling of coming home washed over her, maybe more so than even when she'd returned to the cabin.

Jason waved to her from the bottom of the hill, sitting on the steps that led up to the dining hall. The dining hall was a log structure with a wide wrap-around porch with swings and rocking chairs gracing its weathered wooden planking. A huge stone fireplace hunkered at the far side of the building, its chimney reaching up toward the darkening sky. The place was charming and inviting, worn and weathered, but not a bit dilapidated or old. She lifted her hand in a quick wave, paused one more moment to take in the familiar sight, and hurried down the hillside.

JASON LOOKED up at Bree waving from the hilltop. A surge of emotions swept through him. A longing for carefree childhood days. The friendship. The laughter. Until it had all disappeared on that one fateful day. They had both lost so much that day, and he rarely let himself think about it. That summer had changed his life. He'd become more focused. Decided for certain that he'd come back and help his mother with the lodge. That summer had shown him what was important and how life could be so very short.

He pushed all that aside, just glad to have Bree back, if only for a while and not under the greatest circumstances. It was so like her to be the one sister who came back to get the cabin ready to sell. Always responsible. She always claimed it was her middle child fatal flaw.

She crossed the last of the distance between them, her cheeks rosy from the cool air. A broad smile lit her face. "I've missed all this. Even that hill. Though it's a bit steeper than I remember."

"Old age, Breester. Old age."

She punched his arm. "We're the same age. Are you old?"

"Nah, I'm in great shape. Forever young."

"Then that's what I am, too." Her words and the defiant jut of her chin said one thing, but the hesitation in her voice said she didn't quite believe herself.

She did look tired. Good, but tired. Maybe just from the long drive, or maybe from life's trials. He wasn't sure. He looked up at her from his perch on the step. "I was hoping you would really come. I couldn't miss the opportunity to watch you come down that hillside again. It's been a long time."

"Twenty years."

"Well, you're back now."

She reached down a small, gloved hand for him and tugged him to his feet. "Come on. I hear there's some good cooking around here."

"You betcha. Mom's dying to see you. Let's head for the kitchen."

They cut through the dining room. About half of the tables were filled with diners. He mentally counted them as they walked past. Fairly good turnout for midweek. Maybe the extra online advertising he'd been doing was starting to pay off.

He pushed through the swinging door to the kitchen. "Mom, look who I found."

Nora looked up from her cooking with a warm smile. Bree crossed the kitchen and was instantly enveloped in a hug. He stood back and grinned like a fool. So glad to have Bree back here. So glad to see her in his mom's arms again.

For a moment, just a tiny one, it was like everything horrible had never happened.

But it had.

BREE COLLAPSED GRATEFULLY into Nora's arms. For the first time in a very long time, she felt safe and like she belonged somewhere. How could a hug deliver that much to her?

"I've missed you, girl," Nora whispered in

her ear, not voiced as a reproach, more as a fact. "Stand back and let me look at you."

Bree stepped back and smiled at the woman. Nora looked older. Her hair had streaks of gray and was cut in a short, easy-care style. Her face was lined with a few wrinkles, and she looked slightly thinner. But her smile was the same, and her welcome was heartfelt. She bubbled with the same amount of energy as ever.

"When Jason told me you were here... Well, I'm just glad to see you. You've grown up into a beautiful woman."

"Thanks, Nora." Bree didn't believe that remark. She considered herself okay looking. Her curly brown hair refused to be tamed, she carried an extra ten pounds she just could not lose, and every time she caught her reflection or saw herself in a selfie, she could see the haunted expression hidden behind the flecks of gold in her brown eyes. Not beautiful by any stretch of the imagination. Her older-by-a-year-and-a-half sister, Abby, was the drop-dead gorgeous one. Her younger-by-two-years sister, Cece, well she was short, cute, and vivacious, and people were instantly drawn to her. But Bree's ego had been so beaten down in the last few years that she'd take any compliment thrown her way. Eagerly.

"Now, scoot." Nora shooed them out of the kitchen. "As soon as Judy gets back from the supply room, she'll take over the cooking again. You two go out and grab a table and have a nice dinner. I'll be out to chat as soon as I get things under control here in the kitchen."

They threaded their way through the tables, stopping once for Jason to say hi to someone he knew and once when one of the waitresses paused to ask him a question. He looked like a man in his element. Relaxed, friendly, in charge. No longer the young boy who ran errands for his mom and bussed tables.

Jason led her to the same table in the corner that they'd sat at a hundred times before. He pulled out the worn ladder-backed chair for her and she slipped into it. The faded, shellacked wooden tabletop was showing wear, but still looked inviting. A chrome napkin dispenser and chrome-topped salt and pepper shakers sat atop the table. She remembered many nights sitting at a table after the dining hall had closed filling up those shakers and napkin dispensers as she waited for Jason to finish up and come hang out with them.

The waitress came over and took their order, paying curious attention to Bree and devoted attention to Jason. Bree decided on the lodge's famous meatloaf. Jason ordered fried chicken. They both ordered a cold beer.

They sat in comfortable silence for a bit. Bree watched the comings and goings of the diners and marveled at the lake view through the expansive windows across the front of the dining hall. She drank in the familiar sights and sounds and smells. The clatter of dishes. The low voices of the customers who would occasionally break into laughter. The faint scent of Nora's apple pie. She feasted on her surroundings, wrapping them around her like a child clutches her tattered security blanket.

"Still the same?" Jason interrupted her thoughts.

"The same. But different."

"Well, for one thing, there's just the two of us here at our table. Not the whole group." His voice was tentative.

"Yes, there is that," she answered in a low voice.

"Did you two ever work out your differences?"

"Differences is a mighty understated word for what happened." She fiddled with her napkin and avoided looking at him.

"But you're sisters."

"Sisters don't do that to each other."

"They shouldn't. But we were all kids. Kids make mistakes."

"Some bigger than others. Some more easily forgiven and forgotten." She looked directly at him to drive home her point.

"Do you see Cece often?"

How should she even answer that? Admit they'd barely spoken to each other? They'd only seen each other at scattered holidays at their parents' insistence. That it still took her breath away when her sister walked into a room. That no amount of "I'm sorrys" had been able to mend the rift. Ha, it was more than a rift. It was a canyon of pain between them.

She settled on "I rarely see her."

"That's too bad. You two were so close. I thought you'd work it out by now."

"Do we have to get into this? I'm having a hard enough time with this trip back to Sweet River as it is."

"Sorry, Breester." His eyes held hers for a moment. She could see he was truly sorry.

"How about Abby? Do you see her?"

"Abby. Another story. She's busy with her life and her job. Runs with a fast, partying crowd. I don't see her often either. We don't have much in common anymore."

"So, now that your parents... are... gone." He paused and looked directly at her, his eyes full of warmth and kindness. "Will you and your sisters see each other?"

"Maybe, but I doubt it. My mom's insistence was the only thing that drew us together anymore. And that wasn't very often anyway."

The last thing she wanted was to spend the evening rehashing painful old memories. "So when did you decide to come and help your mother run the lodge? Oh, and what's your sister, Beth, up to these days?"

He grinned at her sharp U-turn of topics. "Short version. Came back here after getting a degree in business with an emphasis on hotel management. I really enjoy working here. I do a little bit of everything. Keep the books. Clear the snow. Jason of all trades." He grinned.

"And Beth? Does she work here too?"

"No, she's a teacher in town. Though she does help out here in the summer. She has two boys. I adore them. Ten and eight years old. They have me wrapped around their little fingers."

"So she's married?"

"She's actually divorced. I don't know if you remember him from the summers you were here, but she married Scott, the star quarterback. She was probably dating him by then when you were here? Anyway, he's a real jerk. Good riddance."

"I remember him." She'd always thought he was a bit full of himself. "I'm sorry, though. Divorce is tough." She knew how hard being married to and then divorcing a jerk could be.

"It was tough on her and the boys. Scott still tries to cut in and run her life, but she doesn't let him get very far. And she's dating Mac McKenna now. Doubt if you remember him. He left town after high school. He's a great guy. Good for Beth."

"And what about Beth's friend... wasn't her name Sophie? They were always together."

"Sophie took over her parents' art gallery in town after they passed away, but now she's singing with Chase Green."

Bree snapped her fingers."I thought she looked familiar. I saw a video of him singing with a new woman, but I couldn't figure it out before. Wow, small world."

The waitress interrupted by bringing out their meals and pausing to flirt with Jason. Of course, any woman with eyes in her head would want to flirt with him. A good-looking, kindhearted man was hard to come by.

When the waitress left, Bree said, "I see you haven't lost your touch with the ladies."

"I have no idea what you're talking about." Jason flashed a boyish grin.

"Yeah. Right."

While they ate, Jason regaled her with stories of the lodge and the people who stayed here. The regulars who came year after year. The townies who came for loud, party-filled weekends. One family who rented the entire place each summer for a huge family reunion. The weddings and receptions they hosted here now, with the guests of the weddings filling up the cabins. She could see how much he enjoyed working at the lodge.

"I guess your Mom enjoys having you help run the place."

"I think so. Remember Jim? The old guy that helped her with everything? He retired right after you left. Well, that last year. I finished college and I just kind of stepped in and took over what he did plus some of the business side."

"Do you enjoy it?"

29

"I do."

"It looks like you've expanded quite a bit. But somehow, it still has its same homey feel."

"Well, I put my business degree from Colorado U to good use. Mom was glad to turn all the financial stuff over to me. She never did enjoy that part of owning the lodge. She's a people person. With some changes, the lodge started showing a much better profit. We updated the inside of the cabins. Put in a new dock and swimming platform."

"For the few people foolish enough to brave the freezing water." She could remember plunging in the lake, middle of the summer, and how it took her breath away with the cold.

"Yes, those crazy kids." He grinned.

"You seem very contented here."

"I am happy here. I can't imagine doing anything else, or living anywhere else."

Bree envied him his contentment. She wondered what it would be like to be so happy with your life, so satisfied where you were. She didn't think she'd ever felt that. Not even in the middle of her marriage to Brian, not even when her son, Cody, had been born. There was always the overlying feeling of what if. But she'd thrown herself into motherhood, and for years her whole life had revolved around raising Cody and trying to keep Brian happy. She'd failed at both and was all alone now. A thought that was her constant companion, like an aching back or a nagging headache, always in the background of every moment of every day. And sometimes, when she couldn't keep the loneliness at bay, she'd crawl into bed for a few days and wallow in self-pity. Not that it helped.

She looked across the table at Jason, glad to have him back in her life again. She'd felt an instant connection between them since the first day she'd met him. He must have felt the same way because he'd befriended her that first summer and never wavered in his always there for her attitude. He'd never acted like he wanted anything more. She reached across the table and covered his hand with her own. "You're a good friend."

His eyes twinkled when he said to her, "I'm a patient friend, I'll give you that. I've waited a lot of years for you to come back and play with me."

She laughed then. A true laugh. Something she hadn't done in she didn't know how long. It startled her, and the tiniest feeling of being alive again crept through her. He squeezed her hand,

and the pressure of it sent a surge of happiness through her.

"Welcome back, Breester."

His words were welcoming her back to Sweet River Falls, but she felt like maybe, just maybe, she was welcoming the real Bree back.

Just then Nora came out of the kitchen with a cup of coffee clenched in her hands and sank down on a chair beside them. "Looks like everything is under control. Not a bad night for mid-week. The lodge is almost full, too."

"And the next four weekends out are booked up completely," Jason added.

"Sounds like business is doing really well." She looked at Nora.

"Jason here has been a godsend. He has a head for numbers, something I was more than happy to turn over to him." Nora reached out and patted her son's hand. "It's nice to have help running this place too. Not to mention having both my kids live in the same town as me. And my adorable but mischievous grandsons."

Jason smiled at his mom. Bree felt a momentary pang of jealousy, for the closeness of the Cassidy family, for Jason and Nora's obvious contentment with life. For the life she once thought she'd have and now knew would never happen. And surprisingly, a fleeting longing for the closeness she used to share with her sisters. She drew in a deep breath. "I guess I better be heading back to the cabin."

"Jason, you drive her back to her cabin."

"Of course." He pushed back from the table. "Come on, Breester."

She stood and took his offered hand, then turned to Nora. "Thanks for having me."

"You come back anytime. You're always welcome."

They crossed the dining hall with its mostly empty tables now. A young guy cleared tables with a clattering of plates as he filled up a gray bin propped on one hip. A cute, dark-haired waitress stopped near him and said something that made him blush. Jason just rolled his eyes as they walked past.

He led the way out into the soft evening light toward his truck. She paused for a moment to look at the moonlight dancing across the lake and the brilliant display of twinkling stars above them.

"I've missed having you here, Bree." His low voice rumbled around her.

"I missed you too." She sighed, willing him

not to carry the conversation any further into dangerous territory.

He turned to look at her. "I've missed *all* of you. Everyone split apart and I rarely saw any of you."

"I just couldn't face coming down anymore. It just hurt too much."

"Twenty years is a long time. You know, Bree, I'd been friends with Peter since kindergarten. You didn't just lose your boyfriend when he died. I lost my best friend."

"Jason, I can't do this now..." She turned, scurried to his truck, and climbed inside.

CHAPTER 3

B ree woke up early the next morning with the sun peeking through the glass panels of the French door to her bedroom. The door opened out to a stone walkway that connected the bedroom she'd shared with Cece with the bedroom Abby had to herself. The benefit Abby had of being the oldest child. That, plus Abby always got her way, anyway. She was just like that. She expected to get her way and got it.

She sat up in bed and stretched. She had a lot to do today. Make a list of all that needed to get done. Go to the hardware store for paint and supplies. Ignore the memories Jason had stirred up last night by bringing up Peter's death.

She still missed Peter with his curly blonde

hair and dancing sky-blue eyes. Or she missed what they'd had together, while it lasted. Her first love. She'd dated him for three years. She missed him and grew angry at herself whenever she caught herself doing it. And hated him. Hate being the dominant emotion. She'd never forgiven him and never gotten over him.

She shoved the memories away. Time to start her day. But first things first. She needed coffee.

She slid out of bed and pulled out some jeans and a hoody from the suitcase she'd thrown on the other twin bed. Within minutes she was ready to leave, with her contacts in, her hair pulled back in a hasty ponytail, and her laptop bag in hand. After she found a decent cup of coffee, she'd stop by the grocery store and pick up some food and coffee for the mornings.

Bree wasn't sure how many days she'd spend down here. She'd taken some time off from the catering business she'd started two years ago. Jolene, her assistant and all-around miracle helper, had promised to handle her phone calls and deal with any future bookings. Her business could handle her being away for a while. Jolene was very capable and could handle the work during a slow time. Besides, Bree hadn't taken time off in the two years since she started her business. Not that this trip was her idea of a relaxing vacation.

Yesterday she'd headed straight to the cabin and hadn't gone into town. Today she pulled her car onto Main Street and looked around. So much the same. Pretty storefronts lined the street. She wondered if her favorite old haunts would still be here. Stepping out of the car, she looked up and down the street. So many memories flooded back.

She ignored them. All of them.

She scanned the nearby storefronts and found a cute shop that boasted the best cup of coffee in Sweet River Falls. Perfect. And internet access. Double perfect. She entered Bookish Cafe and was greeted by a friendly woman who looked vaguely familiar.

"Good morning. Welcome."

"Hi. I've come for the best coffee in Sweet River Falls."

The woman smiled. "That's what they say. I'm Annie, the owner."

"Annie, Nora's friend, right?"

Annie looked at her closely. "You're Jason's friend, Bree, aren't you?"

"I am."

"So are you staying at your parents' cabin?"

"I'm here for hopefully just a few days. I'm getting their cabin ready to sell."

"I'd heard it was going on the market soon. A lovely cabin. I was so sorry to hear about your parents. They were wonderful people. They came here often."

She never knew how to react when people expressed their sympathy on her parents' deaths. Sometimes she just gave a brief smile and nod, and sometimes the tears threatened to flow.

She luckily could just nod with a weak smile this time. So Annie knew her parents. Not surprising in a small town like Sweet River Falls. She wished she'd spent more time with her parents and not shut them out of her life. Regrets. Always regrets. She always thought she'd have time to work it out, at least with her parents. But that chance had been taken away. Quickly and completely.

She turned her attention to a display of pastries by the coffee bar and changed the subject. "Oh, and maybe a danish."

"You can order at the counter and there are comfortable chairs upstairs if you want to grab some internet." Annie nodded at the laptop bag Bree carried.

"Thank you."

She grabbed her coffee and danish and climbed the stairs. A beautiful view of the Sweet River flowing behind the building caught her eye. She walked to the window and looked down on a walkway threading its way along the stream. She added the walkway to her growing well-that-is-new list.

She turned and settled into a chair and opened her laptop to check her business email. The internet had been turned off at the cabin. The coffee was rich and dark, and the internet connection quick. She'd found herself a new favorite spot in town. Then she realized once she put the cabin on the market, she'd have no reason for favorite spots in Sweet River Falls anymore. She'd just close the door on that chapter of her life.

She finished her coffee—and it was all it promised—ran her errands, and went back to the cabin to tackle the job at hand. After walking around for an hour with a pad and paper, listing off everything that needed to be done, she decided it was time for a break.

She tugged on her coat and gloves and

headed to the large wooden swing her father had made and placed beside the lake. The quiet of the lake wrapped around her. Of course, it was winter and the middle of the week. Though, as she remembered it, the lake was still peaceful even with the crowds in town in the summer. She frowned. She had no idea if that was how it still was here at the lake. Maybe it was busy and crowded now. Who knew?

She frowned again. She really didn't know much about it. It seemed strange to be back here, sitting in that same swing—though maybe her father had rebuilt it and it wasn't the very same one—and yet, feeling so disconnected from the place.

Today the wind blew gently, chasing tiny ripples across the surface of the water, which splashed soothingly against rocks at the edge of the lake. She sat and stared, lost in thought with memories crashing through her mind.

"Hey, Breester."

She turned at the sound of Jason's voice. "Hi." It was good to see him standing there, pulling her out of her melancholia. There was no need to spend the next days railing against the fates and hashing out old wounds. That was *not* what this trip was about.

"I came to see if you wanted to come over to the lodge for a bit. Maybe grab some cocoa?"

"Ah, you remember my weakness for the lodge's hot chocolate." She smiled. "Thanks, but I don't think so. I have a lot of work to do."

He raised an eyebrow. "And I can see you're just seizing the day with that to-do list."

"I *did* work. Now I'm taking a break. But I need to get back to it."

"How about I come by with the truck later this afternoon and I can help you pick up any supplies you need from the hardware store."

Bree thought of the long list she'd made of repairs that needed to be made to the cabin. "I will take you up on that offer."

"Good. I'll be by in a few hours then."

"Thanks, Jason."

"You betcha." He walked her back up to the cabin and waved as he disappeared around the corner. She heard his truck start and the crunch of his wheels on the gravel. Then silence surrounded her again. And memories. The quicker she got started on whatever needed to be done, the quicker she could escape the place, once and for all.

She pressed her lips together, threw open the door, and walked back in to face the cabin.

Bree was grateful she'd taken Jason up on his offer of help. They'd filled up the whole back of his truck with the supplies she needed from the hardware store. They headed back to the cabin where he helped her unload all the things she'd purchased.

"You've got your work cut out for you." Jason stood inside and eyed all the supplies they'd piled into the great room.

"I know." She grimaced. "I don't know how I'm going to get all this done in one week."

"One week?" He laughed. "I doubt it."

"Well, that's about as long as I had planned to stay."

"Well then, I guess I'm just going to have to help you."

"No, you have your hands full over at the lodge."

"I should be able to spare some time."

She realized she did need help to get everything done, and even though it was against her nature to accept help, she did, and gratefully. "Thanks. I appreciate that." She set down the last bag with paint brushes, masking tape, and carpet cleaner. "How about I make you dinner tonight to pay you back for all your help? I'm a pretty good cook."

"That would be great. Let me go check in on things at the lodge and I'll be back."

"Okay, I'll see you then. And really, Jase, I do appreciate all the help."

"It's no problem. I'm enjoying spending time with you again. See you soon."

She opened the fridge and looked at the food she'd bought, trying to decide what to make for dinner. She pulled out some chicken, fresh veggies, and salad makings. With a bit of seasoning, she turned it into what she thought would be a nice meal.

She'd always had a knack for picking out spices that blended well and food that went together. She loved plating it so it looked special and appetizing. Presentation was at least fifty percent of the meal as far as she was concerned. Her catering business had grown out of her love for cooking and presenting it in a festive style. Her business had really expanded in the last months, thank goodness. She needed a way to support herself, and motherhood wasn't the most impressive item on a resume for finding a job these days. Her dad had loaned her some money to start the business, and she'd been proud to pay him back after only ten months.

The phone rang while she was putting together dinner. It startled her. She hadn't had a landline in years. She walked around the counter and snatched the phone off the cradle.

"Bree. What are you doing down at the cabin?" Abby. Her sister's voice filtered through the lines.

"Seeing what needs to be done to put it on the market."

"By yourself?"

"Yes, by myself."

"Well, you should have asked me. I would have come with you. I probably could have made time next month some time. No wait, I have that big presentation next month and that conference I'm going to."

Bree knew her sister well enough to know that when the next month after that rolled around, that month would be too busy too. "Abby, why are you calling? How did you find out I'm down here?"

"I called your work number, and what's her name, that woman that works with you, she told me."

"Jolene." Abby had met Jolene twice when

she'd flown through Austin on business trips. Obviously, Jolene hadn't really hit her sister's radar. But then not a lot of people who weren't movers and shakers ever did stick in Abby's consciousness. "Why were you looking for me?" Bree asked again.

"I was wondering when the estate stuff is going to be finished. I found this wonderful investment I'd like to throw some money into."

"I'm doing the best I can. It takes time. And the cabin needs to be spruced up before we put it on the market. A few minor things, and it will show much better."

"Can't we just sell it as is?"

"We could, but without spending too much money, we can probably get a better price for it."

"Will it take long?"

She sighed. Hadn't her sister just asked why she hadn't waited until she could help? An insincere offer at best. "I'm doing what I can, Abby. I'm here for about a week. But then I have to get back to my catering business."

"You could hire someone to fix it up."

"Abby, I don't have that kind of money right now. Everything I earn goes to keeping a roof over my head, or back into my business."

"Well, money's tight for me too now. Cece never has an extra dime to her name. So I guess we'll just have to let you fix it up."

No other offer of help with the work. No offer to pay for the supplies. Typical Abby. "Okay, that's what I'll do. Fix it up. I'll let you know when it goes on the market." Bree hung up the phone. She was positive Abby, with her flashy sports car, fancy condo, weekly maid service, and recent vacation to the Caribbean, had a different definition of money is tight than she did.

Before long she heard a knock at the door and Jason came in, carrying a bouquet of flowers. "I swiped them from the delivery of fresh flowers that came to the lodge today. I'm tight with the owner. She won't mind." He winked.

"Thanks, they're lovely." She poked around in the cabinets until she found a vase. Her mom had always loved to pick wildflowers and scatter them around the cabin in vases. She was forever planting more flowers even though they had such a short growing season here. She'd collected a wide variety of vases from mason jars, to silver vases, to expensive hand-blown glass, to the chipped pottery vase Cece had made in grade school.

"Wow, something smells great." Jason came up behind her. He smelled of soap and a clean scent aftershave.

"Hope you like it." Bree fiddled with the salad makings.

"I'm sure I will."

"Well, I can't really compete with Nora's cooking."

"I know you were always one of the few people Mom would trust in her kitchen. Thank goodness she finally found Judy to help her out. She was trying to do everything herself at one point. Anyway, I thought I heard you opened a catering business."

"I did and it's doing pretty well. I do like to cook up fancy food. I've been catering a lot of parties and some small weddings."

"Do you like it?"

"Yes, I do." That part of her life was good, even if the rest was in ruins. She was good at this catering thing.

Jason reached around her and swiped a stick of celery she'd been ready to chop into the salad.

"Hey."

"Thanks." He grinned at her. "You wouldn't want a man to starve waiting for his dinner, would you?"

"Of course not." She shook her head, then flashed him a smile. "Do you eat at the dining hall every night?"

"Well, I have my own cabin at the edge of the property separated from the other cabins by that small grove of trees. Remember it? It's one of the older cabins, but I've fixed it up. It has a small kitchen, so I do cook sometimes. Most of the time I eat at the lodge or at Mom's. She's started letting Judy run the lodge's kitchen more without hovering all the time."

She handed him a stack of plates and silverware. "Here, go set the table. Dinner will be ready in a few minutes."

They ate their dinner, catching up on news and what they'd been up to in the last years. Jason regaled her with stories about happenings around town. When they finished their meal, he helped her clear up the dishes. "Do you want to go for a walk?" He set their plates on the counter.

"I'm beat. How about we go sit on the swing with a bottle of wine?" She pointed to the bottle of wine on the counter.

"That sounds great."

Jason rustled around the drawers and found the corkscrew to open the cabernet. As she rinsed the dishes and slipped them into the dishwasher, he reached over her head and snagged two wine glasses. She grabbed a blanket her mom always kept on the back of the couch, and within minutes they were headed down to the swing.

Bree settled onto the swing, and Jason sat beside her. She spread the blanket across them to ward off the crisp air.

"You're turning into a city girl. This is almost balmy weather for us."

"Not for me. Though I read this is a warm front for you. They're predicting a rain storm tonight and maybe changing to snow." She wouldn't mind seeing snow again. Didn't see much of it in Austin, though they had gotten a dusting of it last winter.

As if the universe was agreeing, a roll of thunder rumbled in the distance.

"I guess we're going to get that storm they predicted."

"Feels like it." Jason leaned back and poured them glasses of wine.

Bree took the glass and sipped. One thing

she'd learned with her catering business was how to pick out a good bottle of wine. Many of her customers wanted her to provide the wine with their catered events, so she'd learned a lot about it in a short time. Luckily she'd met a man who had recently opened a wine shop near her home. He'd taught her a lot and gave her a good discount on wines she bought from his store. She'd been surprised how helpful other small business owners were if she just learned to ask for help.

"Where'd you go, Bree?"

"Hm? Oh, I'm still here. Mind is just wandering."

"Are you thinking about what it used to be like here at the lake?"

That couldn't have been any further from her mind. "No. I try not to think about those years."

"Not even the good times?"

"The good times were way overshadowed by the bad ending."

"Peter made a mistake. A big one."

"About as big as you can get, as far as I'm concerned." Her heart pounded, and the familiar surge of hurt and anger poured through her.

"I'm sorry you got hurt."

"Me too." Hurt repeatedly by every man she'd ever let into her heart. Let the pity party begin. She swore she was going to get over the whole feeling sorry for herself thing. Soon.

Thunder rumbled and grumbled in the distance, rolling over the mountain peaks. "I should have told you." Jason sighed. Regret touched the corners of his eyes. "I'd known for just a few days. If I had said something, maybe it would have all ended differently. I was just so torn between my loyalty to Peter and my friendship to you. I took too long to make up my mind. I actually headed over to the cabin to talk to you—"

"You knew and didn't tell me?" She hadn't expected that twist.

"I was coming to tell you that day... that day when it happened. I got to your cabin and you and your parents were rushing out to the car. I called but you didn't hear me." He looked down at his hands. "I found out later where you were heading. To the hospital."

He paused and looked at her with tortured eyes. "I've always felt so guilty. Like maybe I could have prevented it all from happening."

So he'd known, too. Of course, he had. He

and Peter told each other everything. Another man, another betrayal. Such was her life.

"I swear I was coming to tell you. You were the most important person to me. The one I felt I owed the truth to."

That made her feel a little better, even if he'd been late in coming to the decision to tell her.

"I promise I'll never keep anything from you again. You can trust me."

She looked at him, searching his face, his eyes. She nodded. But still, she was unable to make herself a participant in this game of remembrance. Instead, she poured herself another glass of wine, pretending the pain in his eyes didn't tear at her heart.

Jason, though, didn't seem to have her qualms about strolling down memory lane. No matter how hurtful those memories were. "I got back home and mom told me Peter had been hurt. By the time I got to the hospital, he'd died."

"Jason, I can't go there."

"Not after all this time?"

"No, not even after all this time."

"I'm sorry, Bree. I thought it might get easier for you as the years went by."

"Well, it didn't. Since I have to face it again and again, year after year when..." She sucked in a breath of the storm-laden air. "New topic."

The wind struck up an almost violent whirl around the lake, matching the twirl of pain racking through her at the memory of that night. The breeze chased white caps across the water. She'd always liked to sit by the lake and watch the storms come in. The fury of the wind, and the power of the waves.

Big drops of rain started to splotch down around them. Lightning cracked nearby, splitting the evening with its silver-white flash.

"We better head inside." Jason stood and reached down a hand. He hoisted her to her feet, and without any more warning, the skies let loose, dumping cold, icy rain on them. He grabbed her hand and they raced through the storm. She tugged open the French door and they slipped inside. Jason shook his head and drops of water sprinkled from his hair. He laughed a deep-bellied, life-is-good laugh, chasing away the echoes of their sober conversation.

The laugh was like magic to her soul. Soothing. Easy. Comforting. "I'm going to go change. Strip off your shirt and I'll throw our things in the dryer."

"You just trying to get me naked? Well, half-naked?"

"In your dreams, buddy." She laughed and went to her room to put on dry clothes. The easy banter buoyed her spirits, chasing away the ghosts.

She slipped off her wet clothes and toweled her hair. The curls rebelled by dancing all around her face. Whatever. She shook her head. She quickly slipped on dry clothes and picked up a towel for Jason. She paused at the door to her parents' bedroom. With a resolute push, she opened the door and walked over to her father's closet. There she rummaged through until she found a pair of sweatpants and an old flannel shirt of her father's for Jason to wear. She pulled the shirt to her face, inhaling the scent. She swore it still smelled faintly of her father's aftershave. Maybe this wasn't such a good idea.

Quit being silly.

She headed back to the great room with the clothes and towel clenched firmly in her hands.

Jason stood in the window and watched the storm turn to a mix of rain, ice, and snow. The icy drops bounced off the worn wooden planks on the deck.

He shouldn't have brought up Peter. He shouldn't have. But he'd hoped that somehow things had gotten better. He'd hoped... he didn't know what he'd hoped.

He just hated how so many lives had exploded that one fateful day.

He wished Peter were still here. First he'd yell at him, then he'd hug him, then he'd... well, there was no use wishing. Life threw curves and you learned to deal with them.

He'd lost so much in his boyhood. His father had died. His best friend had died. Didn't take a psychologist to tell him that was probably the reason he didn't let a lot of people get close to him now. He had friends, just not real close best-friend type friends. He did lots with his family. He was fine with it. Happy with his life.

Mostly.

Bree turning up here had brought up long-forgotten feelings. The easy way they could talk to each other. How he could just always be himself and she accepted him. He remembered back to when, years ago, he'd finally convinced himself to ask her out.

Only his timing had been rotten because that very day Peter had come over and told him that *he'd* asked Bree out. Peter and Bree had quickly become a couple. Though Jason had always had the feeling that Bree cared more for Peter than he did for her.

Sometimes the choices he'd made and his unwillingness to take a risk haunted him. The amount of time it had taken to get up the nerve to ask her out.

If only he'd asked her out first.

What would have happened?

Would Peter still be alive?

CHAPTER 4

S he entered the great room to find Jason looking out the window. His back was cut with strong muscles leading up to wide sturdy shoulders. The thin boy she'd known had grown into a well-built man. He turned when he heard her, and she noticed his muscular chest. Darn good looking...

She tossed the thoughts aside. Kind of. "If you slip off your jeans, I'll dry those too."

He gave her the eye. "You want to see me in my boxers?"

"Again, I say, in your dreams, mister." She handed him the sweats and the flannel shirt. Go change in the bathroom. I'll dry the clothes."

He came out from the bathroom, dressed in

her father's clothes. She was okay with it. She really was. Really.

She plopped their wet things in the dryer and headed back out to the great room.

"No cable service, but why don't you pick out a DVD from the bookcase? We could watch a movie while your clothes dry and wait for the storm to blow over."

She was pleased to see Jason grabbed Casablanca. Good choice. "Start the movie and I'll grab us another bottle of wine. I'm not dashing out in that storm to get the one we left out there." She opened the wine, took out two new wine glasses, and settled down beside Jason on the couch. They drank their wine, watched the movie, drank some more wine, and then put in It's a Wonderful Life... even if it wasn't yet the Christmas season.

A POUNDING noise startled Bree awake. She blinked a few times, then opened her eyes to the hard, flannel-shirt-covered chest she was sleeping on. Jason's arm was draped protectively around her. Light drifted in through the windows, but she couldn't wake up enough to figure out the banging noise. She shook her head to clear it. Stayed up way too late. She ran her hand through her hair and pushed off Jason's chest.

The banging continued.

The door.

Someone was at the stupid door. She looked at the clock and saw it was already eight o'clock. She never slept this late and was sure Jason didn't either. Too many movies and a bottle of wine.

She got up and stumbled toward the door, looking down at her wrinkled clothes. She got to the door and yanked it open. This time it opened almost easily, causing her to have to catch herself to keep from falling backward.

There in the doorway stood her greatest fear.

The person she'd done her best to avoid whenever possible for over eighteen years.

Petey. Looking like the spitting image of his father.

Cece's son.

Cece and Peter's son.

CHAPTER 5

J ason walked up behind Bree and stared at the young man standing there. For a moment he thought he was seeing things. Peter had come back to life.

The young man was the first to recover. "Aunt Bree, I didn't know you were here."

"I... uh..." Bree stood grasping onto the door, a dazed expression on her face.

He'd called her Aunt Bree. This just had to be Peter's son, Petey. Had to be. He'd never met him, but there was no doubt about it.

"I wanted to come see the cabin one last time before... before you guys sell it. I... I didn't know anyone would be here. I saw the car and didn't just want to use my key."

"Does your mother know you're here?" Bree seemed to recover a bit.

The young man squirmed. "Not exactly."

"How not exactly?"

"Well, I didn't tell her. She thinks I'm at school."

"Mountain Grove College, right?"

He nodded.

"Well, come inside." Bree stood aside to let Petey in.

Jason couldn't quit staring at Petey. He reached out his hand to the young man. "I'm Jason... I was your father's—"

Bree cut him off and frowned at him. Jason had no clue what he'd done wrong.

"Petey, go call your mother and tell her you're here. I'm not keeping it a secret from her. Use the landline." Bree nodded toward the kitchen area, and Petey crossed over to the phone with reluctant steps.

Bree turned to Jason. "He doesn't know." She whispered the words.

"Doesn't know what?"

"He doesn't know anything about Peter and me. Just that Peter died before he was born. I didn't want you saying something..."

"What was I going to say? Hi, I'm your

father's best friend and he cheated on your aunt?"

Bree flashed him a quick look. "Just... be careful what you say."

"Got it." As if he'd do anything to make the situation worse. He turned around and headed to the kitchen. If he didn't get a cup of coffee soon, he was going to say something he regretted, and it wasn't going to be anything about Peter and Cece. It was going to be about how Bree should trust him.

He'd promised her that she could trust him, but he was her best friend and he hadn't told her about Cece and Peter soon enough. So maybe it would take a while to build that trust.

BREE COULD TELL she'd made Jason mad, but she wasn't sure how. All she'd wanted to do was to make sure Jason knew that Petey knew nothing about the whole Peter sleeping with two sisters mess. The family had long protected him from the truth. He had no idea why Bree stayed away. He probably just thought she wasn't much of a family person.

And that was the truth.

At least it was now.

"She's not answering." Petey hung up the phone.

"Okay, then. We'll try again later." Bree crossed to the kitchen to find Jason busy making coffee and obviously ignoring her. "How about I make us all some breakfast?"

"That would be great. I'm starving." Petey perched on a barstool next to the counter.

"I'll just have coffee, then be on my way." Jason continued making coffee and rooted around the cabinets looking for mugs.

"They're in that cabinet." Bree pointed.

He grabbed three mugs and set them on the counter.

Bree's cell rang, and she snatched it from her pocket. "Hello?"

"Mom?"

"Cody. Is everything okay?" Her son rarely called her. He didn't even answer often when she called him.

"I was wondering... could I come and visit you for a bit? I... well, Dad's out of town for two weeks and I don't think his new girlfriend is very excited to be here babysitting me, as she calls it."

"You know you're always welcome to come visit." Or stay forever. But she didn't say that.

"I could book a plane to Austin. Dad said he'd pay for it. Pretty sure his girlfriend asked him to."

"What about school?"

She heard him pause. "Well, I finished up almost all my credits for graduation, didn't I tell you that? I'm just doing two online classes and I'll be finished. So I can work on my coursework there with you."

No, he hadn't told her that. She hadn't known. So much she didn't know about him anymore.

"Well... right now I'm in Sweet River Falls working on your grandparents' cabin. Getting it ready to sell. Would you like to come here?"

"Yes. That'd be great. I've never been."

She heard a bit of accusation in his words. Maybe. Or maybe she was just overly sensitive.

"And another surprise. Your cousin, Petey, is here."

"Cool."

"Okay, book your flight to Denver and let me know when you're arriving. I'll pick you up."

"Okay, thanks, Mom."

Bree hung up the phone, her mind reeling. Cody was coming to visit. Even if it was just because Brian's new girlfriend had banished him.

"Cody's coming?" Petey looked at her.

"Yes."

"You think I could stay a few days? I haven't seen him in forever."

"Of course you can, but how about school?"

"We have a four-day break."

"Okay, but even if you are in college, you still have to tell your mother you're here."

The cabin phone rang, and she walked over to grab it off the wall. "Hello?"

"Bree?" Cece's surprised voice came across the line. "What are you doing at the cabin? I saw I had a missed call from there."

"I'm here getting it ready to sell."

"Well, why did you call?"

"I didn't call. Petey did."

"Petey? Why is he there?"

Bree handed the phone to Petey. "Your mother wants to talk to you." She wasn't about to get in the middle of this one.

She headed over to Jason, who held out a cup of coffee to her. She took a sip and looked at him gratefully. "I'm sorry." She kept her voice low. "I... I was just thrown for a loop when Petey showed up. And I wanted you to know that he doesn't know anything about... the mess. I shouldn't have—"

"It's okay. I get it." He looked at her closely. "You doing okay? You've had quite the series of surprises today."

In typical Jason fashion, he was finished being hurt that she'd been so short with him and was worried about her.

"I... I don't know." She didn't know. She was just numb.

Her cell phone pinged, and she looked at it. Text from Cody. Ten a.m. flight.

"Mom wants to talk to you." Petey held out the landline handset.

She walked over and took the offered phone, her mind spinning from all the calls. "Yes?"

"Listen, Petey said Cody is coming there, too."

"He is."

"I think I'll come up in the morning."

Bree closed her eyes for a moment. Cece here too. The hits just kept on coming. It wasn't like she could say her sister couldn't come to the cabin. Cece had every right to. But why now? Why when *she* was here? "You don't need to. The boys are fine here with me."

"I want to," Cece insisted.

"Fine. Cody is flying into Denver tomorrow."

"Why don't you give me his flight information and I'll pick him up, then we'll both head up there?"

She didn't really want to do that, but it was an hour or so to the airport, then another hour or so back. She could be busy getting the cabin ready so this whole nightmare could be over sooner. Maybe she could even get it finished and she and Cody could fly to Austin for a while.

"Okay." She gave her sister the information, reminding herself to text Cody that it would be Cece picking him up.

"See you tomorrow."

Cece might have just meant that as harmless small talk, but it sounded like an ominous threat to her.

CHAPTER 6

Nora looked up as Jason walked into the kitchen at the lodge. He was hours later than he usually showed up to help. She'd noticed his truck wasn't at his cabin this morning. He hadn't shaved yet, and she'd swear he was wearing the same shirt he had on yesterday. She frowned but kept her thoughts to herself."Good morning."

"Hey, Mom." He walked over and leaned a hip against the counter. "Guess what happened?"

She didn't really know if she wanted the details of why he'd been out all night...

"So, Cece's son Petey showed up at the cabin. He..." Jason paused, his eyes haunted. "He looks just like Peter."

She remembered that haunted look. It had been etched on his face for years after Peter's death. Now it was rearing its ugly presence again. "I saw him a few times when he was a young boy. He did look just like Peter. What's he doing here?"

"He said he wanted to come see the cabin before the girls sell it."

"I bet Bree was surprised to see him."

"You could say that." Jason shook his head. "Then Bree's son called and said he was coming, *and* Cece called and now she's coming."

Nora paused and frowned again. "How's Bree handling all that?"

"Well, she's thrilled to see her son. I take it she doesn't get to see him often. He lives with his father." Jason picked up a cinnamon roll from the platter on the counter and took a big bite.

"Did she and Cece ever work things out?"

Jason swiped at his mouth. "Nope. And she's made it clear she doesn't want to talk about what happened. I tried."

"Maybe she's just not ready to talk about it."

"Mom, it's been like twenty years."

"There is no rule book for how long it takes

us to get over it when someone hurts us so deeply. Both Cece and Peter hurt Bree. They broke her trust."

"And her heart." Jason finished the cinnamon roll in one more huge bite. "I've got to run. I'm going to get my work finished, then I want to go back to Bree's and help her with the cabin."

"And run interference between her and Petey?"

"That, too."

She watched while Jason headed out of the kitchen. He still hadn't mentioned not coming home last night, but he was a grown man...

She'd seen the way his eyes lit up when he saw Bree again. She'd seen that same look so many years ago when he was young. He'd never asked Bree out, but maybe he hadn't wanted to take a chance on ruining the close friendship they'd had. But, as his mother, she could tell he had more than just-friends feelings for Bree. He'd had them back then, he had them now. Even if he wouldn't admit it to himself.

Beth Cassidy and Mac McKenna sat at her kitchen table finishing up takeout from Antonio's. The boys were at Nora's for the night. With her busy schedule, Mac running his tavern, and the boys' busy schedules, they rarely had time alone these days.

Mac sat back from the table. "Antonio never disappoints."

"It was good, wasn't it? I know I said I'd cook for us, but I got tied up at school with some stuff." She was always getting tied up with something or other. She needed to learn to say no. Like how she'd dropped out of the mayoral race. She needed to simplify her life and somehow find more time to spend with Mac. She wanted to, she just didn't seem to be able to make it happen.

Mac seemed restless tonight, not his usual relaxed self. He fiddled with the knife in front of him, then set it down.

"Everything okay?"

"What?" He looked at her."Sure."

"How about I clean up the table, and let's go sit by the fire."

"I'll help." Mac rose and began to pick up the containers of food. He usually would have been chatting with her, telling her about his day.

But tonight they cleaned up the kitchen silently. She wondered what he was thinking about but left him alone with his thoughts. She'd already asked if he was okay. He'd talk when he was ready, she'd learned that much about him. And so much more. She enjoyed just having his company by her side.

She cleared the plates and they went in and settled on the couch. She scooted right next to him, and he draped an arm around her. "This is nice." He kissed her forehead.

"It is." The room was lit with only the dancing light from the fire draping a cozy ambience around them. A *quiet*, cozy ambience. That rarely happened in her house with her rowdy boys.

"You know, I've been thinking." He turned slightly to face her.

"Yeah? What about?"

"We don't get to see each other enough."

She sighed. "I know. I was just thinking the same thing. We both are so busy, and the boys..."

He took both her hands in his and squared off facing her. "Beth, you know I love you, right? I'm nuts about your boys, too."

"I'm pretty crazy about you, myself." She smiled at him.

"Well..." He paused, then suddenly pushed the coffee table away from the couch and dropped to the floor on one knee. "Will you marry me?" He held out a ring in his hand.

"Marry?" Her heart raced and she could barely choke out the question.

"Yes, you know. Like wed. Marry." His eyes narrowed. "Move in together. Be a family."

She stared at the ring in his hand, the diamond sparkling in the firelight. "But we live in different towns. And the boys..."

"I would move here. Mountain Grove is only twenty-thirty minutes away."

"My house is too small for all of us." Her mind darted from obstacle to obstacle.

"We'll buy one together. I was thinking out of town a bit. Maybe near the lake, or up in the mountains."

"Are you sure? I mean... the boys... they're a handful." Her voice quavered, and her pulse roared through her, making her words sound muffled.

"I am *so* sure. I've never wanted anything more in my life."

"Oh, Mac." She threw her arms around his neck and he pulled her close. "Yes, I'll marry you."

He kissed her then, softly and gently. He pulled back and slipped the ring on her finger. "You've made me the happiest person in the world."

No, she was pretty sure that she was the happiest person in the world at this moment. She blinked back tears. "I do love you, Mac McKenna."

He slipped back up to the couch and pulled her close. "And I love you, too. We're going to have a great life together."

She leaned against him, her mind whirling, and held up her hand to look at the diamond, sparkling in the firelight. She needed to call her best friend, Sophie, and tell her the news. And sit the boys down and talk to them. And tell her mother.

But right now, she wanted nothing more than to sit here in the firelight and let Mac hold her. A lone tear escaped and trickled down her cheek. A tear of joy and happiness.

"I didn't mean to make you cry." His deep voice rumbled against her.

She turned her face to him. "I'm just so incredibly, completely happy."

"Me, too."

He kissed her forehead again, and she snuggled in closer, wanting to savor this moment for all time.

CHAPTER 7

B eth and Mac headed to the lodge to pick up the boys. He held her hand firmly in his as they entered. They headed to the dining room and found the boys having breakfast with Jason.

"Hi, Mom." Trevor looked up from gobbling his stack of pancakes.

"Hi, boys. Where's Grams?"

"She's in the kitchen." Connor waved a fork toward the kitchen.

"You two going to join us for breakfast?" Jason motioned to the chairs beside him.

"In a minute." She turned to Mac and slipped off her gloves. "Why don't you sit? Order me a stack of pancakes and some bacon, okay? I'm going to go talk to Mom."

He winked at her."Sure thing."

Jason stared at her for a moment. He glanced at her hand, his eyes widened, then he grinned. "Come on, sit down." He got up and clapped Mac on the back. "Give her a moment with Mom."

Beth cocked her head toward the boys and Jason nodded back. She needed time to tell them but wanted to speak to her mother first.

She hurried into the kitchen.

"Mom, got a sec?"

Nora turned toward her. "I do if you can talk while I finish up these pie crusts." Her mother stared at her for a moment, put down the rolling pin, and wiped the flour off her hands. "What is it?" Her eyes filled with concern.

"I... have some news."

"I know. I can feel it."

"Of course you can. It's that weird Mom connection you have." Her face felt like it would break from her wide grin. "Mac and I... he asked me to marry him." She held out her hand.

Nora looked at the ring, then pulled her into her arms. "I'm so happy for you."

"I am, too." She stepped back. "Oh, and by

the way, Jason knows. He spotted the ring on my finger. I still need to talk to the boys, though."

"Well, I'm sure they'll be thrilled. They adore Mac." She dusted more flour from her hands. "The crusts can wait. I'll come out and join all of you."

They headed back to the table and Beth sat next to Mac. He looked at her expectantly. He even looked a bit nervous. For some reason that tickled her. He was most nervous about how the boys would react.

"Boys, I have some news."

Connor and Trevor looked at her. "What?" Connor asked.

"Well, Mac and I." She smiled at Mac. "We're going to get married."

"Whoop!" Trevor let out an exclamation and jumped to his feet. "Really?"

Connor looked from her to Mac. "So does that mean we're all going to live together?"

"It does."

"Okay, that's cool." Connor went back to eating his breakfast.

Mac laughed.

"Told you," she said to Mac. "No big deal."

"Congrats to both of you." Jason reached

over and shook Mac's hand. "Now that I can officially say something."

"You don't miss a trick, do you?" Beth rolled her eyes at Jason.

"Your face was flushed. You had this dopey grin on your face. No way I could miss that. You were practically screaming the news."

She smacked him on the arm.

Trevor frowned. "Mac's gonna squeeze into our house with all his stuff?"

"We're going to look for a new house." Beth watched to see how the boys reacted.

"Will I still get my own room?" Connor asked.

"You will," Mac assured him.

"Okay, that's cool."

She was glad that all their plans were "cool."

Trevor came over and draped an arm around her, leaning close. "I like Mac," he whispered in her ear.

"I like him too," she whispered back, her heart swelling with happiness.

Nora smiled at her from across the table, nodding slightly.

Beth wanted to jump up and dance and twirl around and sing and... she *had* to call Sophie as soon as breakfast was finished.

CECE WAITED NERVOUSLY at the entrance as all the passengers filtered by. She hadn't seen Cody since her parents' funeral. Not that she'd seen him often before that. Bree had only shown up at family things when their mother finally guilted her into a trip. And that had only been every few years or so. Sometimes less than that.

She glanced at her watch. She wanted to grab Cody and hurry to Sweet River Falls before dark.

She was worried that someone might let it slip... Well, that someone might say something that Petey didn't need to know.

She sighed and cocked her head from one side to the other, trying to release the tension strangling her.

Then she saw Cody. He lifted a hand in a small wave as he approached."Hey."

"Cody, good to see you." She gave him a quick semi-hug, even if they weren't really a hugging family. At least not anymore. "You ready to go?"

"Yep, just have my backpack and this duffle."

"Okay, let's head for Sweet River Falls." She led the way to the car.

After battling through traffic, they finally broke away and headed into the mountains. The sun shone brightly against a clear blue sky, though she'd heard they were predicting a storm. Whoever "they" were.

"So... Petey will be glad to see you."

"Yep."

"It shouldn't be much longer."

Cody didn't answer but just looked out the window.

She finally drove down the final stretch of road and headed right to the lake instead of taking the route through town. She pulled up in front of the cabin and turned off the engine. And just sat there staring at the cabin. It was so strange that soon it wouldn't be"their" cabin anymore. She slowly got out and stretched, pretending she wasn't wound so tight she was afraid she'd explode like a jack-in-the-box.

Cody climbed out and stared out at the lake, then turned and looked at the cabin. "It's... wow, I can't believe she never brought me here." His voice was low with a hint of hurt threaded through it.

"Yes... I..." But what could she say? That she

was the reason Bree had never come back here?

He set his backpack on the ground and pulled out a camera. She watched as he put the camera to his eye and took some shots of the lake and the mountains in the background. He slowly lowered the camera and glanced at the screen on the back of it.

The door of the cabin opened, and Bree hurried out. She threw her arms around Cody, wrapping him in a hug."Oh, Cody. I'm so glad to see you."

Cece was betting there wasn't a hug waiting for her from her sister.

"Hey." Cody pulled back from Bree's embrace.

Bree looked at Cece, her eyes filled with... what? Anger? Regret? Anxiousness? Cece ignored the look... or at least tried to. "Hi, Bree."

"Hi." Bree picked up Cody's duffle and headed back into the cabin without another word.

So this is how it was going to be. Well, at least she'd be here to protect Petey. She hurried into the cabin to give Petey a hug—because it appeared it might be becoming a family thing again except between her and Bree.

CHAPTER 8

B ree stood at the kitchen sink washing dishes. She'd actually pulled them out of the cabinet and pretended they needed washing. Anything to keep busy. She splashed her hands into the soapy water and glanced over at Cody fiddling with a camera. That was new. Something he'd picked up since he'd been gone.

There was so much she didn't know about him anymore. Things he didn't tell her about his life. Like the not-so-minor detail that he'd almost finished his high school credits and was only doing two online classes to finish up.

For once she was glad Brian had a series of young girlfriends. Especially because this one didn't want to be in charge of watching Cody while Brian was out of town. Score one for the mom.

She watched Cody as he concentrated on the camera, scrolling through pictures on the back of it. The kitchen light bounced off his jet black hair. He'd gotten that from his father. He'd gotten her golden brown eyes, though. And one of her dimples.

She'd give anything to go back and change things. Anything so he would have stayed with her and not moved to go live with Brian. She missed him so much it sometimes made it almost impossible to breathe.

But he was right here in the cabin with her now, and she planned on enjoying every single minute of it.

Even if she had to share it with Cece and Petey.

She glanced over at Petey sitting at the table with Cece. They were sorting through stacks of old magazines and paperwork. At least that was some help in getting the cabin ready to sell.

She really couldn't imagine how she was going to work side by side with Cece for the next few days. Maybe she could think of errands for her sister to run. Errands that would take a long time and take her far away for most of the day.

Maybe she could think of a supply she absolutely *needed* that couldn't be found in Sweet River Falls. Maybe it would take Cece all the way to Boulder or Denver...

Cece looked up from the table and directly at her.

Bree turned her head away and focused on washing the dishes that didn't really need washing or her attention.

JASON PULLED his truck into the drive at the cabin and saw another car there with Colorado plates. Should be Cece and Cody. He climbed out of the truck, not sure what he was going to see when he walked in the door. Hopefully, it wasn't a war going on...

He knocked on the door, and Petey opened it. It took his breath away for a moment to be looking straight into the clear blue eyes that looked so like Peter's. Sometimes the pain of missing his best friend was a stabbing knife to his heart. He took a deep breath.

"Come in." Petey stood aside.

Jason walked inside and saw Cece sitting at the kitchen table. Another young man—it must be Cody—lounged against the counter, fiddling with a camera.

"Jason, hi." Bree sounded overly enthusiastic to see him. "This is Cody, my son."

He reached out a hand and Cody shook it with a firm grip. "Glad to meet you, Cody."

"Hey." Cody nodded.

"Mom wanted me to come over and see if you guys wanted to eat dinner at the lodge tonight. I tried calling, but the phone is out."

Bree walked over, picked up the landline, and sighed. "Yep. It is. I'll get someone out to look at it tomorrow."

"Last time it was squirrels in the attic. They chewed the wire." Cece stood and walked over to him. "Hi. Long time."

"It has been." The awkward tension in the cabin crackled through the air. Bree stared at him with a look that dared him to be friendly with Cece. He ignored Bree's look and hugged Cece quickly.

Cece's eyes shone with gratitude, and she flashed him a brief smile.

He turned to Bree. "I don't have your cell phone number, so I couldn't call it to invite you." Back to the safe subject of the phones. Good plan.

"Here, hand me your phone. I'll put it in. Especially if we're not going to have the house phone." She walked over and held out her hand.

He handed her his cell and watched while she tapped in her number. He glanced at it as she gave it back. She'd labeled it Breester. He grinned at her and slipped his phone back in his pocket.

"So, what do you say? Dinner at the lodge?"

"Sounds good to me." Cece looked at Bree.

"I... I guess so. I was so busy painting today, I didn't really think about making something for dinner." Jason wasn't sure he believed that. She was one of those people who could throw together a meal from almost nothing. She'd done it when they were younger and everyone wanted a late night snack, and he was sure she could look in those cabinets and pull together something. But she probably wanted to escape the tension in the cabin.

He didn't blame her. He was kind of ready to escape it, too.

"I'll drive. It will be too dark to walk back to the cabin later." Cece reached for her keys.

"I'll ride with Jason." Bree walked over, grabbed her coat, and waited by the door.

"Okay, come on, boys. You're with me." Cece slipped past Bree.

They all headed outside into the darkening night. Bree tugged the door closed and locked it, then walked quietly over to his truck and climbed inside.

He got in and started the motor. "You doing okay?"

She stared at him, her expression grim. "Just peachy."

CHAPTER 9

They all threaded their way through the tables to their old regular table in the corner of the dining room. A long wood-planked table that had seemed to expand to whatever size they'd needed. Nora came bustling up to them. "Cece, I haven't seen you in forever. Come here." Nora wrapped her in a hug.

Bree wasn't sure she was okay with that. Nora was *her* special person, not Cece's. She knew she was being petty, but she just didn't care.

Nora turned to Petey. "Haven't seen you since you were a boy, but I'd recognize you anywhere. You're the spitting image of your father." She turned to Cody. "And you must be Bree's son."

"Nora, this is Cody." Bree motioned to her son.

"Glad to meet you, son."

"Good to meet you, ma'am."

Bree smiled at his good manners. She was used to his usual "hey" remark when he met people, but he must have known that Nora wasn't a "hey" person. At least some lessons she'd taught him had stuck with him even while he hadn't lived with her.

"Sit, sit. I'll have the waitress bring over menus. I've got to check on a few things in the kitchen, then I'll join you." Nora turned and waved at a couple coming into the dining room. "Look, there's Hunt and Keely." She motioned them over.

They crossed the room, and she didn't miss how Cody's eyes lit up at seeing the camera hanging around Hunt's neck. She needed to talk to him about this new passion of his. Something he'd picked up since... She pushed the thought away. He was here now.

"Why don't you two join us for dinner? There's plenty of room," Nora offered.

"We don't want to impose," the woman said.

"Nonsense, plenty of room." Jason nodded at the table. "Hunt, Keely, this is Cece and her son, Petey. And this is Bree and her son, Cody."

"Nice to meet you." Hunt smiled. "If you're sure, we will join you."

Jason turned to her. "Hunt and Keely are from Comfort Crossing, Mississippi, but they're renting a cabin here for a year while Hunt works on a photo shoot of the area.

"It's so beautiful here." Keely took a seat and Hunt sat down next to her.

Cody quickly moved around the table and took the seat on the other side of Hunt.

Cece sat down, and Bree took a seat as far away from her as possible.

Cody nodded at the camera Hunt had placed on the table. "Canon?"

Hunt smiled. "Yep. I've tried them all, but I keep coming back to my trusty Canon."

"Mine's a Canon, too. Not as nice as yours, though."

"So you shoot?"

"I'm learning. Took some photography classes in high school, then took one at the community college over the summer."

"We'll have to go out shooting together."

"Really?" Cody's eyes widened. "I'd like

that." He looked at Bree. "That's okay, right, Mom."

He said it more as a statement than a question.

She nodded. She hadn't seen Cody this excited about something in a long time.

"Great. Got a cell phone?"

Cody nodded.

"Let me have your number." They exchanged numbers as the waitress came up with menus.

Nora's choice of adding Hunt and Keely to the table seemed to have been a good one. It broke the tension, and the conversation drifted from topic to topic. Cece remained rather quiet, but that didn't bother Bree. She'd rather her sister didn't say anything at all. She didn't want to be tempted to go off on her and tell her exactly what she thought about her. Something Bree had held inside all these years, ever since the day she'd stormed out of the hospital after learning that Peter had died.

Cece had tried to apologize a number of times, but Bree wanted nothing of it. You couldn't just apologize for sleeping with your sister's boyfriend... and then getting pregnant.

Bree turned away from Cece and smiled at

Keely. "So, Hunt's a photographer. What do you do?"

"I manage a cafe back home with my sister. It was my parents' and now my sister and I run it. She's managing it alone this year while I'm out here with Hunt. Well, she runs it along with Becky Lee. Becky Lee's been working at the Magnolia Cafe forever and I'd trust her with anything. Between the two of them, they're doing fine."

Hunt looked at his wife and smiled. "Keely's been running the cafe since she was just out of high school. It was time for her to have a break. She's a writer. She's been writing some articles for regional magazines and websites while we're here. And she's also started writing a novel."

"Really? That's exciting." Jason looked at Keely with admiration. "I've never met a real live author."

Keely blushed. "Well, it's my first novel. But I'm certainly enjoying writing it. My background is in journalism writing, so I have a lot to learn."

The conversation continued around Bree, but she didn't really tune in to very much of it. Except when Cody spoke. She listened to his every word.

They finally finished dinner after what seemed an eternity and rose from the table.

"I'll call you about a photo shoot. We'll do it in the next day or so." Hunt shook hands with Cody.

"Bree, you riding back with us?" Cece stood in front of her as if daring her to say no. Or maybe daring her to say yes.

"I can run you home," Jason offered.

"No, you don't need to. Cece is headed that way. I'll ride with her." But she wished there would have been some graceful way she could have accepted his invitation...

But she was going to make darn sure she got the backseat in Cece's car. One of the boys could sit up by Cece in the front.

Petty, she knew it. And she didn't care.

THEY PULLED into the drive at the cabin and Bree frowned. Another car besides hers sat in the driveway.

"Wonder whose car that is?" Cece turned off her car.

They all climbed out, and the boys headed to the cabin. She got out slowly, giving Cece plenty of time to go ahead of her. She watched the three others go through the door and trailed behind them.

She walked through the door and pushed—twice—to close it behind her. Still needed to fix that.

"Hey, sis."

Bree whirled around. "Abby, what are you doing here?"

"I got to feeling guilty that you were here doing all this work by yourself, so I thought I'd come for a few days to speed things up. I had a layover in Denver on my trip back home, so I just changed my ticket."

"Well... uh... great." She wasn't sure how much help Abby would actually be, but she'd wasn't going to turn down the offer.

Then her heart sank. Ugh. All was good except that Abby was going to want her old room, and Bree had planned to put Cece in there...

Cece looked at her. "Looks like we'll be roomies again."

Bree gritted her teeth. This whole trip was veering off the rails.

"Boys, you can have the loft." Cece took charge.

It wasn't Cece's *right* to take charge. "Why don't you share Abby's room?" Bree challenged.

"There's only one bed in there. There's two in our room. And I really can't face sleeping in Mom and Dad's room."

Bree didn't really think Cece had a right to call it "our" room anymore, but she did fully understand the not wanting to sleep in their parents' room.

"It's only a tiny full bed in my room, Bree. Of course, we can't share it. That's silly when there are two beds in your room." Abby picked up her suitcase.

And, of course, Abby would claim one room to herself.

"Fine." She'd just stay up late until Cece was asleep and slip into the room then. She'd get up early. There'd be no time for the late-into-the-evening talks they used to share.

Just sleep.

CECE LAY in bed listening to her sister move about the cabin in the great room. She knew Bree was just avoiding her. She didn't blame her, but she wished anything that somehow, by some miracle, things could go back to how they were before. When she and Bree were best friends.

Before she'd made such a stupid mistake.

But she never let herself really regret sleeping with Peter, because out of that, she got Petey. And she'd never, ever regret having him. He'd been the biggest blessing in her life.

She sighed, punched her pillow, and rolled over.

Life was complicated.

CHAPTER 10

Nora hurried into Bookish Cafe the next morning as soon as the breakfast rush was over at the lodge. She couldn't wait to tell Annie about Beth and Mac's engagement.

Her friend looked up from where she was sorting books onto a shelf and waved her over. "This is a surprise."

"I had errands in town, thought I'd stop by for a few minutes."

"I'll grab us coffee and let's go sit upstairs."

She followed Annie up the stairs. A few people were scattered around the loft, using the internet on their laptops or sipping coffee. She and Annie settled into two overstuffed chairs overlooking the river.

"So, anything special you wanted to chat about?" Annie raised one eyebrow.

Nora laughed. "Well, maybe. You know me so well."

"I can tell by the look on your face. Spill it."

"Well... Beth and Mac got engaged."

"No kidding. Good for them. He's a good man, and he seems to make her very happy."

Nora took a sip of coffee. "And he's great with the boys. I'm just so happy for her. I was afraid after Scott divorced her, she'd never take a chance. Then Mac came around and... well, like I said, I'm happy for her."

"Any wedding plans yet?"

"Not yet. She did say she wanted something small. At the lodge. That's all I got."

Annie sighed. "That sounds wonderful."

"I have other news," Nora continued. "Did you know that Bree Stuart is back in town?"

"Yes, she came by the other day to grab some internet."

"Well, her sister Cece showed up with her son, Petey. I swear, he looks so like Peter that it's uncanny."

"Well, that must be awkward for everyone."

"It is. Bree's son is here, too. They came over for dinner at the lodge last night. Thank goodness Hunt and Keely stopped by because it helped break the tension."

"You know, I always thought that Jason had a bit of a crush on Bree." Annie mindlessly traced her finger along the rim of her cup.

"I know he did. I think he still does."

"Really?"

"I've seen the way he looks at her. I don't even know if he knows he feels that way about her. He's closed himself down since losing his dad, then losing his best friend. All that at such a young age."

"Well, maybe she'll be just the one to open him up to possibilities again."

"Maybe." She came this close to telling Annie about Jason not coming home the other night, but he was an adult and was entitled to his privacy.

"I wonder how long they'll be here?"

"Just until they can get the cabin ready to sell. Jason's been helping some."

"Well, maybe the girls will have some time working together and will talk. Maybe they'll find some way to bridge the hurt."

"Maybe. But from the way Bree was acting last night at dinner, I'm not so sure." She'd seen Bree's furtive looks at Cece and her deliberate exclusion of Cece in any conversation.

Some wounds took a long time to heal.

Some never did.

BETH TOOK her planning hour and went to the teacher's lounge. Sophie and Chase had a big concert last night, so Beth had waited until today to call and tell her the news.

She tapped on Sophie's number and listened to the rings.

"So, it's about time you called to tell me." Sophie's voice came through loud and clear and accusing.

"What do you mean?"

"The news that you and Mac are getting married."

Beth sat down. "Wait. How do you already know?"

"Let's see. Nora told Annie who ran into Hunt and told him. Then I called the gallery and Hunt was there setting up another series of his photographs. His first words were 'Isn't that great about Beth and Mac.'"

"I would have called last night, but you had

a concert. Then I wasn't sure how early you'd be up."

Sophie laughed. "Well, small towns. It's hard to get ahead of the gossip. But honestly, I'm thrilled for both of you."

"Thanks. I'm sorry I didn't get to tell you personally." Beth smiled at another teacher who came into the lounge and got up to walk over to the window. "And you'll be my maid of honor, right?"

"Of course." Sophie paused. "Well, when are you planning on getting married?"

"We thought in a month or so. We don't really want to wait."

Sophie let out a long sigh."Chase and I are headed for a European tour in three weeks."

"For how long?"

"It's a couple of months, at least. Chase has planned a vacation in Europe for the two of us in the middle of all of it. Our agent is trying to tack on a few more concerts. But we could cancel our vacation part and come home."

"Nope, not happening. Let me talk to Mac and I'll get back with you on the dates. Because I'm not getting married without you. Just saying."

"You better not. But, hey, I've got to run. We

have a recording scheduled. Call me soon and let me know what your plans are."

"I will." Beth slipped her phone in her pocket. She hated to wait three or more months to get married. She'd promised Mac that they could get married soon.

She frowned. Then she smiled.

She had just the plan.

CHAPTER 11

J ust as Bree figured, Abby wasn't much help with the actual work needing to be done to get the cabin ready to sell. She insisted she couldn't paint and kept asking a million questions when she started going through paperwork in the files, so Bree had to stop and look at each piece of paper she questioned.

Cece had actually offered to box up their parents' clothes. That was one task Bree wasn't ready to tackle, so she gratefully turned it over to her sister. Even if it did mean Cece was here at the cabin all day.

Bree painted the bathroom, then tackled the linen closet. She took a handful of linens in her arms and headed to where they were collecting a giveaway pile. She paused at her parents' bedroom doorway. Cece sat on their parents' bed holding their mother's favorite yellow sweater. Tears rolled down her cheeks.

A war raged through Bree.

A part of her, from a distant memory of herself, wanted to rush in and console her younger sister.

The other part, the bigger part, wanted to just quietly walk away.

"Mom, we need you. Got a minute?" Cody called from across the cabin.

The war ended because she'd always choose Cody over Cece. She headed to find out what her son needed, grateful she didn't have to make a decision.

Cody and Petey stood with paint rollers in hand. "We ran out of paint. You said you wanted everything the same color, right?"

"Yes, just this neutral greige color. Supposed to sell better this way."

"So that's what you call this color. In some of the light it looks grey, but when the sun shines in, it looks beige." Cody glanced around the room.

"Hence the word greige was invented."

"We could go into town and get a few more gallons," Petey offered.

"That would be great. I bought it at the hardware store in town. You can get some more mixed to the same shade. Color is on the paint can lid."

Cody snapped a picture with his cell phone of the paint can lid.

"You can take my car." She searched around in the kitchen drawer where they always put their car keys. She'd dropped them in there from force of habit. As she rustled through there, she spotted the spare set of keys to her parents' car. The car that no longer existed anywhere but in bits and pieces in some junkyard, crumpled and broken. She swallowed hard and blinked her eyes. She was not going to cry. Not over car keys. Not over anything.

She snatched her keys from the drawer, slammed it shut, and turned to the boys with a deliberate smile. "Here you go." She handed him the keys and some cash.

"Thanks, Mom. Need anything else?"

"Could you ask at the hardware store if they have more boxes we could have? Or maybe swing by Bookish Cafe and ask Annie?"

"Sure."

"You could also pick up some Mexican at Antonio's for dinner. Just an assortment of stuff. You two choose. Enough for all of us."

"Okay, will do."

The boys headed out the door, and she turned to see what Abby was so engrossed in. She was reading one of the old magazines. Great. That was helpful.

She turned to go back to work.

Cece came out into the great room. "I'm going to take a break on sorting out Mom and Dad's stuff." Her eyes were red from crying, though she had a fake I'm-just-fine smile plastered on her face.

"How about we all three work on the kitchen?"

"What needs to be done in the kitchen?" Abby asked.

Only *everything*.

Bree turned to her sister. "We need to box up things. We can donate some of the canned goods to the food pantry. We'll leave out some plates and glasses to use while we're here, but we can box up a lot of the pots and pans. The placemats and tablecloths. I assume we're going to donate anything that's in good shape?"

"I'd like some of Mom's vases." Cece's voice held a just quiver.

"Fine. Take what you like." Bree nodded.

"You think anything is worth much? We could sell it?" Abby added.

"You got time for that? Because I don't." Bree stood with her hand on her hip. No way she was going to be roped into a yard sale. There were people around town who could use some of Mom's cookware. That was good enough for Bree.

The three of them headed to the kitchen, opening cabinet doors. Then they all three stood back and stared. It was going to be a bigger project than she'd planned. She sighed. "I'll get some boxes."

They sorted through the pantry items first, throwing away an amazing amount of expired food. Then they packed up non-perishables to donate. Bree kept a shelf of a few things that she could use to make quick meals, like the pasta and spaghetti sauce.

Abby grew bored of the work and went back to sit at the table, pretending to sort through paperwork. Bree was pretty sure her parents had every receipt and manual for every item they'd ever bought for the cabin. Even items that were long gone. Surely Abby could handle that much, right? They'd keep the manuals for the appliances for the new owners.

New owners.

It wouldn't be their cabin anymore.

But what did she care? She hadn't been here in years.

And yet, a tiny part of her heart was shredding at the thought of no longer being able to just walk into the cabin. Touch things her mother had touched. Sit on the deck like they'd all done so many times. What she would give to have one more morning sitting out on the deck with her mom and sipping coffee. Or sitting on the wooden swing with her dad, watching the sunset creep across the sky and throw splashes of color reflecting on the lake. She closed her eyes for a moment, either hiding from the memories, or embracing them. She wasn't sure which. She opened her eyes determined to get on with the work.

Out of the corner of her eye, she saw Cece open the key drawer.

And close it.

"How about I pour us all a glass of wine?" Cece went to the fridge and grabbed a bottle of white wine.

"Great idea." Abby looked up from where she was leafing through a magazine. Again. Lovely.

Bree nodded at Cece. "Sure, why not."

Cece poured three glasses, took them over to the table, and sat down next to Abby.

Oh, they were evidently having glasses of wine *and* a break. She reluctantly went over to join her sisters.

She took the offered glass of wine and settled at the end of the table. "Here, at least give me a stack to sort through while we sit."

Abby handed her a stack of crumpled booklets. She sifted through them while she sipped her wine. "Oh, look. Here's the manual for that old radio. Remember? Mom used to play that jazz station all the time while she worked in the kitchen. Wonder where it is now? I haven't seen it."

"It broke," Cece said. "Got knocked off the counter years ago."

For some reason Cece's remark irritated her. Cece knew about chewed phone lines and broken radios. It was obvious she still had come to the cabin.

And *she* was the reason that Bree hadn't been able to come to the cabin. It didn't seem fair. Why hadn't Cece stayed away, and then she could have come to the cabin for all these years?

Though, she knew she wouldn't have. Too many memories. She could still picture Peter standing at the edge of the lake, skipping stones. Or lounging against the deck railing. Or...

She closed her eyes.

Abby rose from the table. "I think I'll go get my nail polish and do my nails."

"Seriously? With all this work to do?" Bree stared at her sister.

"I've worked all day. I think I can take time off to do my nails."

"Except you haven't worked all day." Cece chimed in. "You've been leafing through magazines and *acting* like you're helping.

"You two always gang up on me." Abby's eyes flashed.

"There is no 'us two' anymore," Bree said flatly.

"There would be if you wouldn't be such a self-centered, self-righteous jerk about everything."

"Hey, Abby..." Cece held up a hand.

"No, really. She ruined our family. Ruined everything."

"*I* wasn't the one who ruined our family."

Bree couldn't believe Abby was accusing her of wrongdoing. Her? It was *Cece*. Cece had ruined everything.

"You did. You ruined everything. Cece apologized for sleeping with Peter. Okay, so he was your boyfriend. But we were all young. She made a silly, young girl mistake. You could have forgiven her. Everything could have stayed the same."

A crash came from near the door. The three sisters turned in unison, the first time they'd done something in sync in twenty years.

"Petey..." Cece's voice was hushed.

Mexican food lay all around Cody and Petey's feet.

Petey's eyes burned with anger and hurt. "You slept with Aunt Bree's boyfriend? My dad was Aunt Bree's boyfriend?"

"Petey, let me explain." Cece rose from the table.

"I'm pretty sure there's no explanation for that. So that's why Aunt Bree didn't come around much to family stuff."

Cece hurried across the distance and reached out to touch his arm.

He jerked away. "No, don't touch me. Don't talk to me. You've lied about my dad all these years. Saying what a great guy he was. He wasn't. He was a cheater, just like you."

Petey whirled around and fled out the door. Cece still held her arm outstretched.

Cody stood dazed, the Mexican food splattered around him.

Bree got up from the table. "Way to go, Abby."

"I didn't know he was here." She defended herself. "You *did* ruin things."

"No, she didn't. It was my fault." Cece slowly lowered her arm.

"Great, even when you two aren't speaking you're ganging up on me. It won't ever change." Abby rose and sent a stack of magazines tumbling to the floor with a dramatic sweep of her arms. "You two never did understand me. I've always been the outsider. Fine. Why should things ever change?"

"Abby—" Bree took a step toward her sister.

"Don't bother. I'm leaving. You two finish up what you want on the cabin. Or don't. I don't care. Just get it on the market and let's get it sold."

Abby hurried to her bedroom and Bree heard the door slam, the sound reverberating through the now silent cabin.

Cody looked at her. "Mom?"

"We'll talk. Let me just get this mess cleaned up."

"You think I should go after Petey?" Cody's browed creased.

"I think maybe he needs a little time to process everything."

JASON LOOKED up at the hill between the lodge and the Stuart's cabin and swore he saw Peter standing there. Like so many times before when they'd cut back and forth. He squinted and looked closer.

No, it was Petey up there.

He put down the broom he'd been using to sweep the deck steps and headed up the pathway. He needed a break anyway, right? Or maybe he just wanted to get to know this part of Peter. Peter's son. The son who looked just like his father.

He climbed the hill and walked up to the gazebo. Petey whirled around when he heard him. Jason swore the kid had been crying.

"You okay?"

"I'm great. Just great."

"You don't sound great."

Petey swiped at his face. "I just found out about—" He looked at Jason. "But I bet you already know."

"Found out what?"

"About my father. And my mom. And Aunt Bree."

So somehow the boy had found out. "I did know."

"You knew that my parents were cheaters? That mom lied to me all these years?"

"I don't know what your mom told you, no. But I will say that to wrap all the things your father was up into one word—cheater—doesn't describe him at all."

Petey stared at him then frowned. "So... how would you describe him? Can you tell me more about him? Mom doesn't talk about him much."

"He... he was a great guy. My best friend. He was funny. He was smart. His laugh could bring a smile to everyone's face. He went to visit his grandmother every week, without fail. He was great at sports. Loved to hike. He was the first one every year to plunge into Lone Elk Lake, when the water was frigid. Not that it ever really warmed up."

Petey sat on the bench and continued to look at him.

"He never got sick. He could outrun me in the mile by three seconds. Three seconds."

The boy almost smiled.

"He did make a stupid mistake with Bree and Cece. He was young, but that's no excuse. If any of us could have known how this would have turned out..."

"So that's why Aunt Bree doesn't come around. She hates my mom."

"She doesn't hate Cece. Not truly in her heart. I've always hoped that the two of them could work things out."

"Why would Aunt Bree ever forgive my mom? That's a rotten thing to do to your sister."

"We all make mistakes, son. All of us. Some bigger than others. We do things we regret. That's life. It is."

"So Mom's probably sorry that I was ever born. I'm a constant reminder."

"I doubt that's how Cece looks at you. She loves you. You have to know that."

"Honestly, I don't know anything right now. Everything I thought was the truth... it isn't." Petey looked out at the mountains in the distance. "But I'm glad Aunt Abby blurted the truth. I am. Because now I know. Now I understand."

"Maybe. I'm not sure any of us fully understand. We all made choices that led up to how things turned out."

"I'm just so mad at my mom right now."

"It's okay to feel upset and angry. I'm sure it was a shock. But did you ever make a dumb mistake that your mom forgave you for?"

The corners of Petey's mouth turned up in the tiniest smile. "I did shoplift when I was in high school. I was trying to fit in. It was stupid. Mom made me go to the store and return the jacket. Then I was grounded for a month and she took my phone away."

"So, you were young and made a stupid mistake." Jason looked at the boy. "She still forgave you and loved you."

"But it wasn't as big as Mom's mistake."

"Your mom's been paying for her mistake for a long time. I think it's time she was shown some forgiveness. Anyway, how about I walk you back to the cabin. If there's one thing I've learned, it's no good to run from your problems."

CHAPTER 12

Cece looked up when the door to the cabin opened.

Petey.

She sprung to her feet and hurried over, reaching out a hand, but then dropping it back by her side. "You're back."

He nodded.

She looked at Jason standing beside Petey. "You found him?"

"We were just having a bit of a chat." Jason shifted from foot to foot.

"I don't really want to talk." Petey started to walk away from her.

Jason rested a hand on Petey's sleeve. "Like I said, it doesn't pay to hide from your troubles."

Petey stopped and turned to face her. "You

slept with your sister's boyfriend. Dad cheated on his *girlfriend*. Aunt Bree was Dad's girlfriend. I... I don't even know how to deal with that."

Cece noticed Bree and Cody standing back. And Jason was right here. So it appeared she was going to have to do this in front of everyone. "I was young. Your father was young. We made a terrible, terrible mistake. We broke Bree's trust and her heart. I'll never forgive myself for that."

"I think that maybe I'll just head to the kitchen and leave you two alone." Jason walked away, and Bree and Cody followed him into the kitchen area.

Not that it would give them much privacy, but at least they weren't standing right here while she talked to Petey.

"So I'm just one big mistake in your life." His eyes flashed, full of pain.

Pain she'd put there. Her heart twisted. "No, I didn't say that. You are *not* a mistake. You are the best thing that ever happened to me."

"Right. Except I ruined everything. Aunt Bree can barely stand to be around me. Everyone says I look just like Dad. So I'm a constant reminder to her."

"It's not you she doesn't want to be around,

it's me. And even though Bree was very hurt, I don't regret being with your father. I got you. I'm only sorry it blew up the family in the process."

"Did Grams and Granddad know about it?"

"Yes, I told them."

"So I was the only one in the family left out of the truth?"

"I don't think Cody knew either, but you'd have to ask him. It wasn't mine to tell him."

"Why did you keep it a secret for so long?" Petey scowled. "I should have been told the truth."

"I didn't want you to think less of your father. He was a good man. He was. We just made a mistake. A big one. And as I said, I only regret that Bree got hurt. I will never regret that I had Peter's son. That I had you."

BREE STOOD in the kitchen trying to ignore the conversation going on just a few yards away. She tried *really* hard to ignore it.

Cody had headed up to the loft with his headphones on. Good choice.

Jason stood and rattled around, packing up a stack of pots into a waiting box.

Cece had said she'd never forgiven herself for breaking Bree's trust. Or her heart.

And she had to admire her sister—just a tiny bit—for saying she didn't regret being with Peter because he'd given her a son she adored.

Even though it still made her angry just thinking about the whole affair. She frowned and reached for a glass to get some water. Not that she needed it, she just needed to keep herself busy.

For the first time she wasn't raging angry when she thought about Cece and Peter. Kind of. Her own actions after it had happened had been what tore the family apart. She couldn't really blame that on Cece. It had been her. She'd ignored the family and refused to visit until her mother positively guilted her into a quick trip. And then she'd made sure that everyone knew how miserable she was and what a big favor she was doing them.

She took a mindless sip of water.

How had she become that person?

The one who thought that everything was about her?

"You okay?" Jason asked quietly. "You look... funny."

"Funny?"

"Well, like... you're getting sick or something."

"No, I'm just thinking." She kept her voice low.

"About what?"

"About... well, maybe I'm not as blameless in the mess our family has become as I thought."

He gave her a quick smile. "Adulting is hard, isn't it? Everything isn't as black and white as we sometimes think."

She looked at his kind face, full of empathy more than sympathy. He'd always been there for her.

But she'd deserted him, too. Without so much as a word. What kind of friend does that?

She felt a frown crease her forehead.

She had a lot of thinking to do.

ABBY RETURNED HER RENTAL CAR, checked in for the flight she'd booked—the red-eye—and headed to the gate. She had two hours to kill before the plane departed. She settled into an uncomfortable seat at the gate. Then got up. After aimlessly walking down the terminal, she entered the nearest bar and ordered a drink, mindlessly munching on the nuts the bartender put in front of her.

It wasn't her fault. It wasn't. She hadn't known Petey was there. That he could hear her. She never would have told him the truth. The family had hidden it from him for years. Cece's choice.

But now he knew.

She sighed and took a sip of her drink.

And he knew because she'd lost her temper.

The two of them—Cece and Bree—just brought out the worst of her. They'd always been the unstoppable duo. She'd been the odd man—girl—out. She would hear them laughing and talking in their room late into the night when they were kids. They hadn't offered for her to join them.

But she couldn't change what had happened, and now Petey knew the truth, and maybe that wasn't such a bad thing. She'd tried to get Cece to tell the truth to her son years ago, but she wouldn't listen.

Abby could understand how Cece didn't

want her son to know about her... *transgression*... but the truth had a way of always managing to set itself free.

Okay, she had helped it along a bit in this case.

And she was honest enough to admit to herself that she'd kind of left her family to pick up the pieces after she'd announced the truth.

Oh, well. She couldn't change things. She'd head back home where she couldn't cause any more trouble.

She just hoped Cece and Bree got the cabin ready to sell in a hurry.

She *needed* that money.

BREE WALKED into her bedroom later that evening. Cece stood gathering her things together.

"Are you leaving?" She walked farther into the room.

"I thought I'd move into Abby's room. No need to share if she's gone." She folded a sweater and put it on a stack on the bed. "Petey's leaving tomorrow, though. Has to head back to school."

"So, you're leaving tomorrow?"

Cece turned and looked right at her. Bree's heart raced at the look in her eyes. Hurt mixed with fierce determination.

"I'd like to stay for another few days and help you with the cabin. It's not right that we dumped everything on you." She paused in folding another sweater. "If that's okay with you."

Though it didn't really sound like Cece was asking her permission.

Bree stood for a moment, unsure of how to answer. She needed the help, she did. And for the first time in a very long time, she wasn't anxious to get away from Cece.

"It's okay with me if you stay."

She didn't miss the tiniest smile that flashed across Cece's face before she turned back to gathering her things.

CHAPTER 13

Petey left early the next morning, and Cody went out on a photo shoot with Hunt. Bree and Cece were left alone in the cabin. Bree did her best to pretend it wasn't awkward as a three-legged race in the snow.

"We could finish up Mom and Dad's room so that's behind us," Bree suggested.

"Okay, but I'm warning you, it's not an easy job."

Bree didn't mention that she'd seen Cece crying yesterday while sitting on their parents' bed.

"Well, let's see if we can finish it all today." They grabbed boxes and entered their parents' bedroom. A wash of pain swept over Bree. Flashes of her mother sitting on the bed talking to her. Her dad reaching into his closet to pull out one of his flannel shirts for her to wear while they headed out to sit by the lake on the swing. The sounds of her parents talking and laughing. So many memories swirled around her.

"You want Mom's or Dad's closet?" Cece stood holding a box.

"Ugh. You choose."

"I'll take Dad's." Cece went over and opened the door to their dad's closet. "Do you want anything?"

Bree crossed over to stand beside her sister. "Actually, I think I'll keep a couple of his flannel shirts."

Cece grinned. "You always did love to wear them."

"I did." She picked out two of her favorite shirts and held them up to her face. They still smelled of her father's aftershave. Tears threatened to storm her eyes. She swallowed.

Cece reached out and set a hand on her arm. "I could do it all if it's too hard."

"No." Bree busied herself folding a shirt. "I'm fine." It was only a tiny white lie. She would *make* herself fine. She painstakingly folded each flannel shirt, then set the stack of them on the bed and turned to her mother's closet, swinging open the doors.

That was a mistake. All of a sudden, all the air in the room sucked away. She couldn't breathe, couldn't think. She backed away and sat on the bed as tears rolled down her cheeks.

The bed jiggled and Cece sat right beside her, crying herself.

They both sat silently while their tears ran free. Bree didn't even try to stop them.

"I miss them so much." Cece's voice was barely above a whisper.

"I do, too," Bree answered. Only, she'd missed them for so many years with her stupid choice to cut them out of her life along with Cece. Why had she been so determined that was a good decision? She'd lost so many years, so many days, she could have spent with them. Cody could have gotten to know them better. He could have come here to the cabin with his grandparents. Maybe even worked in town during the summers just like she had. He would have loved that.

Guilt and remorse, mixed with the pain of loss, flooded through her until she thought she might drown in it.

She turned to Cece. "I... I am so sorry, Cece.

Sorry I basically left the family. Sorry I couldn't get over it."

"I'm so sorry for what I did to you. I am." Her eyes shone with fresh tears.

"And I think it's about time that we tried to work things out. Come to a better place. I mean, I'm still mad at you." Bree paused. "No, that's not even right. I'm sorry it all happened. But if I'm being honest, the pain of it is beginning to seep away. I... I wish I would have handled it differently."

"Oh, Bree." Cece threw herself into Bree's arms.

She held her sister then, for the first time in years and years.

And it felt... right.

They finally pulled apart and swiped at the tears on their faces.

"Well, I never thought that would happen," Cece said.

"I'm glad it did. I don't know how things will work between us, but this is better than it's been, right?"

"Even if it did take Mom's and Dad's clothes to bring us together." Cece looked at the open closets. "So you think we should tackle the rest of the bedroom now?"

"Yes, let's do. Let's get more of the past behind us." Bree resolutely walked over to her mother's closet and started packing up the clothes. But not before she set aside her mother's favorite sweater for Cece.

CHAPTER 14

C ece, Cody, and Bree headed to the lodge for dinner that night. Cody could not stop talking about what a great time he had on his photo shoot with Hunt. Something about aperture and depth of field and f-stops. Bree didn't know what it all meant, but she was pleased that Cody was so happy.

They walked into the dining hall and Nora waved from across the room and motioned for them to take their regular table.

Jason came over to join them as they took their seats. "Good timing. I was just going to grab something to eat."

Cody jumped up when he saw Hunt and Keely enter the dining room. "Can I invite them, too?"

"Sure, the more the merrier." Jason nodded.

Hunt and Keely joined them, and Hunt and Cody immediately launched into a discussion of photography. Cece and Keely chatted about the upcoming predicted snow storm.

Jason leaned over and whispered, "So, things going okay with all of you? You and Cece seem—I don't know—less at odds."

"We talked some. I don't know where we are right now, but things are better. At least I think they are." Bree reached for a menu the waitress brought. Not that she needed it. Except to see what the special dessert was tonight. Because she was going to treat herself to some empty calories.

"I'm glad things are better for you two. Have you heard from Abby since she left?"

"Nope. I'm pretty sure she won't call. She was pretty mad when she left, but I think part of that was being mad at herself, too. She has a way of blurting things out, then regretting them later. She has no off switch."

"Well, that was a rough way for Petey to find out the truth."

"It was."

They were interrupted when Nora came over with a bottle of red wine. "On the house for some of my favorite people." She poured glasses, passed them around, and sat down beside Jason. "You heard we have a big storm coming tomorrow?"

"I did. Don't worry. I'll be ready to clear the roads."

"We have that wedding this coming weekend. I'd hate for the weather to mess with that. The bride was so excited about having a winter wedding. Outside, of all things, though we did say we could host it in the main reception area of the lodge if need be. We can move the benches around and bring in chairs. It's a small wedding. It would work."

"Well, if she wants it outside, hopefully she's got snow boots she wants to wear." Jason grinned.

"I really think we should consider the expansion of a conference venue that could be used for meetings and weddings. We have that land at the far side of the property where we'd planned on putting in a few more cabins. I think a meeting venue might be more worth our while."

"I agree. I've done up some preliminary numbers on it since you last mentioned it."

"You have?" Nora smiled. "Well, of course, you have. You're my numbers guy."

"Let me have a bit more time to firm things up, and I'll go over it all with you. Then we can make a decision."

Bree watched the confident businessman, Jason, as he discussed the expansion of the lodge. A businessman in a flannel shirt and jeans.

Nora stood. "I've got to head back to the kitchen and help Judy. We're short a kitchen worker tonight." She headed back to the kitchen.

Bree leaned toward Jason. "You love working here, don't you?"

His eyes lit up. "I do. I love working with Mom, love the people who come here—mostly —and love helping her plan things that help grow the business.

A clatter of broken plates caught their attention. A young waitress stood over a pile of broken dishes on the floor. She fled out of the dining room.

"I better go help." Jason rose.

Bree watched as he expertly spoke to the people at the table who were expecting the food that now sat piled on the floor amongst broken dishes. He promised them a free bottle of wine, a free meal, and that he'd rush their order through again.

She turned to Cody. "I'll be right back." He nodded but barely looked up from his conversation with Hunt. More f-stop thingies.

Hurrying over to where the dish bins were kept, she grabbed one, returning to start cleaning up the broken dishes on the floor. Jason walked up to her. "I was going to get that as soon as I told Mom to rush their order again."

"I've got it. Just need a quick mop up."

"I'm afraid I'm going to have to put on my waiter persona. Penalty of being an owner. Have to chip in where needed. That new waitress seems to have disappeared."

"You go do that. I'll finish up with this." Bree mopped the last of the mess from the floor, then noticed a table nearby with empty water glasses. Without stopping to really think, she went and grabbed an apron from the waitress station along with a pitcher of water.

She spent the rest of the evening helping Jason with the dining room crowd. He slipped past her one time and grinned. "Just like old times, huh?"

Cody came up to her later as she was

clearing a table. "We're finished eating, but you never got your dinner."

"I'll grab something when we're finished. You go on to the cabin with Cece. I'll be back soon."

"Hunt said I could go with him again tomorrow. He's hoping the storm clouds from the snow coming in will make for some good photos. Can I go again?"

It didn't escape her that he actually asked her this time. She smiled. "Of course. I'm glad you're learning from him."

"Okay, see you later at the cabin." She watched as Cody and Cece left the dining room.

She busied herself clearing the rest of the tables and waiting for the last group of diners to finish up.

Nora came out of the kitchen and looked around at the dining room in surprise. "You cleared up all of this? I figured I'd be here for hours we're so short-handed."

"Just that one table left. Do you need help in the kitchen with the dishes? I seem to remember I was quite the expert on dishwashing."

"When you weren't starting water fights." Jason grinned. "Anyway, I have a better idea." He put his hands on his mother's shoulders and turned her to face the door."You go back to your cabin. Bree and I will finish up."

"I can't do that." Nora shook her head.

"Yes, you can. Go. I'll help Jason." Bree nodded agreement.

"I don't know..."

"We need to find more help for the dining room." Jason continued to propel his mother toward the door.

"Preferably ones that don't drop trays of food," Bree added wryly.

Nora laughed. "That, too. Okay, I'm out of here. Thanks, you two."

JASON LOOKED around the kitchen an hour later. The dishes were finished. He'd double-checked to make sure the ovens were off, stove off, and fridge door was locked.

Bree rested on a stool, her faced flushed from the heat in the kitchen. She looked— adorable. She also looked relaxed, and a hint of a smile teased the corners of her mouth.

Not that he was staring at her mouth.

She sat finishing up a piece of apple pie. He walked over, smiled, then pushed a damp curl away from her face and ignored the shot of heat that raced through him when he touched her skin. He jerked his hand away and shoved it in his pocket. "You did good tonight, Breester. We really needed the help."

"I'd forgotten how tiring it is." She self-consciously pushed back more of her hair and set the plate on the counter beside her. "The time goes fast while you're working, but then, it just kind of hit me."

"Let me take you home. You do look beat."

"I don't think that was a compliment." She shoved at her hair again.

"Well, what I meant to say was you look wonderful."

"Much better. So we're all finished here?"

"Yep." And yet he stood there and stared down at her, perched on the stool. He stared at her lips and watched while her tongue darted out to moisten them.

Time froze for a moment, trapped between the days when they were young, carefree kids, and the present.

He reached out to pull her to her feet, her hand lighting a fire in his. She stood in front of him, inches away, the electricity between them impossible to ignore.

He wanted to kiss those lips.

But they were friends. He didn't want to mess that up.

He was almost certain he saw desire darken her eyes. And uncertainty.

Before he could make up his mind to actually kiss her, she turned away. "I'll go get my jacket."

Once again, he was just a little too late...

CHAPTER 15

Cece sat in bed reading. She was too mentally and emotionally tired to tackle more of the cabin tonight. She heard Bree come home and the low tones of her talking with Cody. After a bit, she looked up to see Bree standing in the doorway to the bedroom.

"You jumped right in there to help. Just like we used to do when we were kids."

"It was kind of instinct, I think." Bree leaned against the doorframe.

"Did you ever get something to eat?"

"I did get a piece of Nora's apple pie. So good."

"Jason drove you home, I guess?"

"He did."

Cece sat up straighter. "He likes you, you know."

"What? Don't be silly. He doesn't. We're just friends."

"I see how he looks at you. His eyes do not say friend. They say... more than that."

"You're crazy."

"No, I'm not. He had a crush on you when we were kids, you know."

"He did not."

"Bree, you were always clueless. Listen to me. He liked you then, he likes you now. More than like."

"I think you're wrong." Bree turned to leave.

"Bree?" Her sister stopped. "I've... I've never had anyone look at me like he looks at you. You should give it a chance. He's a great guy."

BREE SAT on her bed in the room she used to share with Cece. She had happily banished her to Abby's room when Abby had left.

Now the room felt... wrong. Like Cece should be in here with her. Chatting. Talking. Laughing.

She was sure Cece was wrong about Jason. He didn't like her like that. He didn't.

Though, there was that one moment in the kitchen tonight. Something had been going on between them. Some kind of magnetic pull.

She'd thought he was going to kiss her.

So she'd stood there like a fool, and he hadn't, so she'd turned away. Maybe she'd misread things.

Maybe she didn't know anything about *anything* anymore.

Just as she started to drift off to sleep, one more thought tormented her mind. Cece had said what a great guy Jason was...

Did she have to worry about Cece going after Jason now?

Not that there would be anything wrong with that, because there wasn't a she and Jason.

He was a free agent. Able to date anyone.

But the thought of Jason dating Cece pretty much strangled her heart.

CHAPTER 16

H unt knocked on the door early the next
morning. Cody bounded to the door
and tugged it open. "Hi, I'm almost ready.
Come on in."

Bree came up to Hunt as he entered the
cabin and glanced around. "Nice place."

"A bit torn up now, with all the boxes."

"Cody said you were getting it ready to sell."

"So far it seems like an endless job."

He shook his head. "I'm sure it is. Has to be
a lot of history between these walls."

He was right. There was so much history
here. So many memories. It seemed impossible
to stuff all that in boxes and make it go away.

Cody came up, shrugging on his winter coat

and slinging his backpack over his shoulder. "I'm ready."

She glanced out the window at the weather, unsure if this expedition was really a good thing. The storm clouds were already gathering in the distance over the mountains.

"I'll keep my eye on the weather. We'll head back to town if it looks like the storm is moving in faster than expected," Hunt assured her.

"Well, I'll be here." Bree looked around the great room, mentally ticking off the list of things that still needed to be packed up in this room. Not to mention they had to figure out the whole furniture situation. Should they try and sell it with the house? Donate it?

More decisions. She was so tired of making decisions.

She watched as Cody and Hunt pulled out of the drive and turned as she heard Cece come into the room. "I've finished up with the bathroom in the master suite."

"You did?" Bree was grateful to have one more thing taken off her plate.

"Yeah, it wasn't as hard as I thought. Not as bad as the closets. Mom had every lotion known to mankind, though. And fifty shades of lipstick, yet I rarely remember her wearing any. I do admit to opening up Dad's aftershave bottle and sniffing it. I miss that scent."

"What did you do with it?"

Cece smiled guiltily. "I put it in my room. Thought I might take it home with me."

"Scents can bring back memories, can't they?"

"They can..." Cece looked at Bree, hesitating. "You know that scent of pine trees? The heavy almost vanilla scent of their bark?"

Bree frowned, but it turned into a smile. "I do know what you're talking about. I hadn't really associated it with vanilla, but, yes, I get that."

"Well... I can't stand that smell..." Cece's eyes clouded.

"Why not?" She frowned again, unsure where her sister was heading with this.

"Because—" Cece looked right at her. "I sat there with my back against that huge pine tree for hours after Peter fell off that cliff."

She paused and sucked in a deep breath. "I worked my way down to him, scrambling over rocks and boulders until I could reach him. I didn't know if I'd find him alive or not."

Bree swallowed, not sure she wanted to hear this.

"But when I got there, he was alive. Barely. I rested his head in my lap and leaned back on this massive pine tree. The scent swirled around me. To this day..." She turned and walked over to the window, staring out at the lake. "I was afraid he would die in my arms. He was hurt so badly. I kept calling for help until my voice came out in croaks. But still I called out."

"Mom said someone did hear you calling for help."

"Hours later, yes. The rangers came and got us. Airlifted Peter to the hospital, but he was already... gone."

"So you sat with him like that for all that time?"

"Yes. I didn't want to leave him alone to... die. So I couldn't go for help. Besides, I never would have made it back out of that ravine by myself. I thought maybe I'd die down there, just like him. I was..." She placed her hand on her belly. "I was so afraid that I'd lose the baby, too."

She could feel Cece's pain. It was like a stab to her own heart. Cece had gone through so much that day.

"Peter was such an accomplished hiker. He

knew how to be safe, not to take chances. How did he slip off the trail?"

"We were arguing..." Tears filled Cece's eyes. "I had just gotten up the nerve to tell him I was pregnant. He stopped in his tracks and whirled around to face me... then the next thing I knew he was losing his balance and he disappeared over the edge of the trail."

Bree remained silent. She'd never heard Cece's version of what had happened that day. What her sister had gone through.

Bree had always made the accident about what it had done to her. How *she* felt. How she'd lost Peter. How the pain of it all had almost crushed her very soul.

"He... died in my arms that day. You know what his last words were?"

She could barely hear her sister now.

"He said to tell you that he was sorry."

Bree rested her hand on the back of a chair to keep her balance. The world as she knew it was exploding around her. Her pulse raced, and the room swam in front of her eyes.

Cece's pain was like a real object in the room. A ton of rocks crashing down on them and burying them alive. Bree wanted to reach out and comfort her sister, but her body wouldn't listen.

Cece turned away from the window and faced Bree. "I shouldn't have asked him to go hiking with me that day. He didn't really want to, but I think he felt obligated since... well, you know, he'd slept with me. By then we both knew what a big mistake we'd made. But I just wanted to be alone to tell him about Petey. Someplace... away from everyone. I was so scared and excited at the same time. But if I'd just told him anywhere, like say in town, or out by the lake. Well, he'd still be alive."

"It's not your fault he died." Bree, finally broken out of her inertia, walked over to stand by her sister.

"Then whose is it?"

"It was an accident. A horrible accident."

"But I asked him to go hiking with me. I blurted out I was pregnant because he was hiking so fast, annoyed at me, and I couldn't keep up with him. I wanted him to look at me. At *me*. And not see you."

"Cece, all these years you've carried this guilt?"

She nodded. "It was bad enough knowing what I'd done to you. It was terrible to add on the guilt of his death. It was like he paid the price for our mistake... but I didn't. I got Petey."

BREE LOOKED out at the gathering snow clouds and checked her watch for the millionth time. Finally she heard the crunch of tires on the drive and Cody came bounding into the house.

"Hey, Mom."

"I was getting worried."

"It hasn't even started to snow yet."

And just like that, big, fluffy flakes started to float down from the sky.

"Okay, well, Hunt got me back before it hit. I'm going to go grab my computer and download these photos I took."

"Are you hungry? I could make you some pasta."

"We stopped and grabbed food at Antonio's before he dropped me off."

"Okay, well, I'll let you work then."

She wandered to her room, feeling off-kilter. So much emotional upheaval in the cabin today. Cece had gone to her room—Abby's room—for a bit. Bree stood and stared out the window at the huge flakes coming down.

She grabbed her coat and pulled on her boots. A walk in the fresh snow would clear her mind.

"Cody, I'll be back soon. Just want to take a walk."

"Okay." He barely looked up from his computer where he was so engrossed in his photography.

She stepped outside into the quiet late afternoon air. The ground already had a wisp of snow covering. She'd forgotten how much she loved walking in the snow. The peacefulness of it. The muffled quiet with only the sound of her footsteps.

She headed down the road, then climbed the path up the hillside. Up to the gazebo. Up to the view of the lake and the mountains. The clouds hung low, wrapping the tops of the mountains in their cloak. She stood there breathing in the fresh air and the scent of the pines.

She paused. She would never feel the same when she caught the smell of the pines. Not after what Cece had told her. So many emotions rolled through her, overpowering her. She held onto the railing of the gazebo, steadying herself.

Suddenly she knew what she wanted to do.

Needed to do. She needed to talk to Jason. He always listened, always understood. He'd always been able to help her sort things out.

She turned and headed to the path down toward the lodge. She looked down at the lodge, covered in a thin blanket of snow, and smiled.

There he was, on the steps of the lodge, looking up at her. As if he'd known she needed him.

CHAPTER 17

Jason looked up from where he was shoveling off the first of the snow from the front steps of the lodge. Bree stood at the top of the hill. She lifted a hand in a wave and headed toward him.

He wasn't really surprised. She loved to walk in the snow. He remembered that about her. He remembered so many things about her. She loved strawberries and croissants. She loved helping her mother pick flowers and arrange them in the bazillion vases her mother had. She loved cinnamon anything. And the color teal.

And walking in the snow.

He put the shovel away, for now, but knew he'd be out again because the snow was really beginning to dump its fury.

"Hi." Bree looked at him.

"Hi, yourself." He could tell something was wrong, but she would talk to him on her own time. That's always the way it worked. "Why don't you come in for some hot chocolate? Get warmed up."

She nodded and followed him into the lodge. They headed to the kitchen where Nora was busy putting finishing touches on the evening's meal.

"Well, hi, you two."

"We came for hot chocolate." Jason pulled off his gloves.

"I've got a pot of it heating on the stove. Figured we might get requests for it tonight. I doubt if we'll have more than just the people here at the lodge for dinner with the storm coming in." Nora grabbed two mugs and pressed them into his hands. "Good thing, because two workers called and said they weren't going to make it in."

"We can help." Bree offered.

"I can't let you work again."

"But of course you can." Bree shrugged off her coat and took the mug of hot chocolate from Jason. "Let me text Cody and let him know I'm staying here awhile so he won't worry and think I got lost in the snow."

"Well, I appreciate it. I could use the help."

Jason knew why Bree was jumping in to help. She wanted to talk, but she wasn't ready. Sometimes she was so easy for him to read. That was fine. She could take her time. They'd talk after the dinner rush.

Once again they worked side by side. He readily admitted to himself he was enjoying every minute of it, not that waiting tables was his favorite thing to do at the lodge, but it was fun to do it with Bree.

The crowd thinned out and Bree finished clearing all but the last two tables of diners. His mom came out from the kitchen. "Judy is going to spend the night with me at the cabin instead of trying to drive home and get back in the morning. You two let us finish up tonight."

"You sure?" Jason had already started untying his apron. He wanted to give Bree a chance to talk before he took her back home.

"I'm sure."

He led Bree out into the lobby area. "You want to come to my cabin for a bit? I can drive you home after that."

"That sounds great." She pulled on her coat.

They headed out into the night. The storm had really hit them full steam while they'd been busy waiting on tables. They walked side by side through the deepening snow. Bree started to lose her balance at one point and grabbed his arm. She kept her hand on his arm, steadying herself as they walked along the path to his cabin. He covered her hand with his own gloved hand.

They went inside and stomped the snow from their boots. He took her coat and gloves and put them on a chair by the door. "I have the fire all ready to go. I'll just light it. Why don't you wander into the kitchen and see if you can find us something to drink."

He lit the fire and watched as the flames slowly ignited the kindling and a plume of smoke rose from the wood. He turned when he heard Bree come back into the room. She handed him a bottle of beer. They clinked bottles in a silent toast and each took a swallow.

He sat back on his heels. "So, you ready to talk now?"

The magical tones of Bree's laughter filled the cabin. "Of course, you know I need to talk."

"Of course, I do." He nodded gravely, then

flashed her a grin. "Come on, let's sit on the couch."

Bree slipped off her boots, and they settled on the couch. She curled her legs beneath her, one hand wrapped gracefully around the beer bottle. He watched as she raised the bottle to her lips and took another sip. His gaze remained on her lips long after she'd set the bottle on the coffee table.

She turned to face him. "So... I think..." She glanced away then back at him. "I think I'm a self-centered, terrible person."

"No, you're not." His response was automatic. She was one of the kindest, most giving people he'd ever met.

"I've always made Peter's accident about me. How it affected *me*. Today Cece and I were talking, and she told me all about those last hours of his life. How she held him until he died. And then still held him. How she was afraid no one would find them and she might lose the baby. I can't even imagine her fear."

He stayed silent and let her talk.

"I was so mad. So hurt. I felt so betrayed. It was all about me and how what they did affected me. I mean... I still think it's terrible that Peter cheated on me. That Cece slept with him. I mean she's my *sister*. But I've come to realize that I've put so much of my energy into this anger. I didn't think about how it affected Cece and Petey. Or how my pulling away from my family affected everyone. I was so self-righteous." She took another swallow of her beer.

"It was a really tough time for everyone." He reached over and put his hand on her knee. "Everyone was scrambling to find their footing."

"But don't you see? I never brought Cody here to Sweet River Falls. He would have enjoyed coming here with his grandparents. I didn't give my parents much chance to get to know Cody. I rarely brought him to any family holiday. All I could think about was how I was wronged."

"And now?"

"Now... now I wish I could have a do-over. I wish I'd spent more time with my folks when I could. I wish Cody could have grown up coming to the cabin all the time like I did. I wish..."

A lone tear trailed down her cheek, and he reached out to brush it away.

"Well, we can't change the past. We can only change the future. But we can learn from our mistakes."

"I hope I have learned. I'm trying to fix things with Cece. I'm trying. But I can't fix things with my parents. It's too late. I have so many, many regrets."

"And somehow you're going to have to find a way to forgive yourself. Move on. Change things." He took both her hands in his. "You're a wonderful, caring woman. We were all young when Peter died. It affected all our lives. The important thing is how we go forward from here."

"I want so many things to change."

"Then change them."

"I'm going to try."

He pulled her close and tucked her against his side, one arm draped around her shoulder. "I'm sure you'll figure out a way."

IT WAS ALWAYS easy to talk to Jason. She loved that. She felt so safe and accepted tucked up against his side, watching the flames dance in the fireplace.

Jason was mindlessly trailing his finger up and down her arm, staring into the fire. His touch soothed her in ways she couldn't put into coherent thoughts.

Soothed her *and* stirred something inside her at the same time. She turned her face up to his. "Hey, Jason?"

"Hm?"

"Were you going to kiss me last night?"

His face broke into a wide grin. "You always were direct."

"Were you?"

"I was. But I spent too long thinking it over."

"So, have you thought about it long enough now?"

He laughed, throwing his head back with a chuckle. "I have. I do think it's time I kissed you."

She raised an eyebrow.

He slowly leaned closer and wrapped a hand around the back of her neck. The warmth of his touch burned through her. She closed her eyes waiting for his kiss. A kiss she realized she might have been waiting for for most of her life.

His lips closed on hers, and she swore she heard singing and bands and fireworks. Her heart pounded so hard she could barely breathe, and heat rushed through her. He finally pulled back and she blinked.

"Wow, that was worth the wait." He grinned at her.

"It was... good."

He laughed again. "It was much better than good. It was fantastic. Perfect. Great."

"Yes, all of those things, too." She smiled at him. "Can I have another one?"

"If you insist."

He kissed her again. And again. They sat and watched the fire with breaks to kiss some more. And some more.

JASON FINALLY PULLED AWAY from her. "I should get you home. It's getting late. I'm going to go out and start the truck and scrape the windshield. You stay in here until I finish."

She didn't really want to leave, but she really should head back. The roads would only get worse as the storm raged on.

Jason kissed her one final time and rose to put on his coat. "I'll be back."

She should really get her boots on and get her coat, but still she sat looking into the fire.

The night had been magical. His kisses ignited something inside of her. Something fascinating and new and... she'd never felt it before. Not with Peter. Not with her ex-husband.

The door opened, and a cold blast of air slammed through the cabin. He closed it with a shove.

"So, got some bad news. The truck won't start. I could go get mom's car and jump it, but really, the roads are terrible already. I'd take you over on the snowmobile, but I have it torn apart in the shed working on the motor."

"I guess we'll have to walk back."

"Breester, it's almost a whiteout out there. I think you should stay until morning. I'd say you could stay at Mom's, but she already has Judy staying in her extra bedroom. The third bedroom she's turned into an office. So... I guess you should stay here. With me."

She swallowed.

Stay.

Here.

In Jason's cabin.

But, honestly, it did make the most sense. There was no reason to risk it on the roads.

"Let me text Cody, so he'll know where I am and not worry."

She typed in her message. Erased it and started again.

Cody, I'm staying at the lodge overnight. The roads are bad. I'll be back in the morning.

THERE WAS no way she was telling him she was staying at Jason's cabin... She watched while the words disappeared into the air. Soon Cody replied with a thumbs up.

Jason knocked the snow off his boots and placed his coat on a hook by the door. "So, how about I open a bottle of wine? We can stay up for a while? Or are you sleepy?"

She wanted to stay up. Sit on the couch... and just let him kiss her. But that might not be the smartest plan.

"I am pretty tired."

"That's fine. Let me make up the extra bedroom for you. It's probably a good idea to hit the sack. I've got to get up really early and start the plow."

And just like that, the magic of the night was over. He made up the bed, gave her an old flannel shirt of his to sleep in, and left her at the door to her room as he headed to his.

He didn't even kiss her good night.

Which was probably a good thing. Right?

It probably would have been a great idea to get some sleep... if only he could actually, you know, fall asleep. He lay in bed and stared up at the ceiling.

What was he doing?

Why had he actually kissed Bree? And, wow, had he kissed her. So many times. It was like he couldn't get enough of her.

But he knew better than this. She was leaving. He'd long ago made a promise to himself to never get in the position where someone would leave him again. Especially leave him voluntarily. It was bad enough when they died and left him...

He shouldn't be breaking his rule. He shouldn't.

Yet visions of her face and her lips danced before his eyes. How was he supposed to have resisted when she asked if he was going to kiss her?

He was weak, that was it. Weak.

He rolled over on his stomach and buried his face in his pillow, wanting to scream. He rolled onto his side and stared out his bedroom window. The snow was still coming down. He had a busy day tomorrow. He glanced at the clock. Correction, a busy day *today*. He groaned and tried to will himself to sleep.

But the minutes kept ticking by, taunting him.

CHAPTER 18

B ree awoke the next morning and looked around, confused for a moment on where she was. The sound of a motor outside the cabin caught her consciousness. She looked down at the flannel shirt she was wearing.

Jason's cabin.

She quickly got up and got dressed. With a brief look in the mirror and some finger combing of her hair, she headed out to the main room. "Jason?"

No answer. She headed into the kitchen. Beside the coffee pot was a note telling her he'd be back to get her soon. He was getting a head start on plowing the roads.

She poured herself a cup of coffee and walked over to look out his window. The snow had tapered off, and a blanket of white covered the banks of Sweet River. It was magical looking. She'd so missed the snow.

She finished the coffee and rinsed the cup. She could certainly pull on her boots and walk herself home. She scribbled a note to Jason and walked outside.

She sank into the snow and realized it was up over her boots. Maybe her whole idea that she could walk back to her place was a bit ambitious. She should wait until the roads were clear, right?

She saw that Jason had plowed the main road at the lodge. Maybe she should go see if Nora needed help at the dining room.

But then Nora would know she'd spent the night here. At Jason's. Yes, they were grown adults and nothing had happened, but suddenly she felt like a high school girl sneaking around.

She trudged through the snow, down the pathway, and headed to the road that cut through the lodge property. When she got to the road, she saw Jason down the road a bit, plowing the snow. She walked down the road toward him until he noticed her.

He pulled up near her, turned off the motor,

and jumped down. "Morning. Did you find your coffee?"

"I did, thanks. I was going to walk back home but..." She pointed to her boots. "It's pretty deep. Did they plow the main road yet?"

"Not yet."

She stood there wondering if he was going to kiss her, but he didn't. He remained a good distance away from her. He tugged off his gloves as if they were the most interesting things to look at in the world.

"I need to get the lodge plowed and shovel the steps to the dining room. Then we'll see if the main road is plowed and I'll get you home."

"I could help shovel."

Jason eyed her. "You sure?"

"Yep." She wasn't really sure. The snow was deep, and she hadn't shoveled snow in years, but at least she could help.

"Shovel is beside the front door to the lodge."

"I'll head there now."

"I've got a few more roads to plow here, then I'll be over." With that, he turned away from her.

She watched while he climbed back on the plow and headed away. She frowned.

No kiss. No smile. No jokes.

Something was off. She could feel it.

She turned and walked to the dining hall, grabbed the shovel and started in. Before long she was hot and tired. Her arms and shoulders ached from scooping and tossing the heavy snow.

Nora came out of the dining hall. "Bree, what are you doing?"

"Shoveling?" Her word came out in a gasp.

"Give me that." Nora took the shovel from her grasp. "You come in and get some coffee or hot chocolate. Jason can finish this up when he gets done plowing."

"I can get this..." She looked at the long pathway to the steps. She'd only cleared the steps and a few yards of the pathway with all her efforts.

"He got a new snowblower a month or so ago. He can use that to clear the pathway. Come inside."

Well, that would have been a good piece of information. She could have quit once she'd conquered the steps...

She gratefully accepted Nora's offer and followed her inside. She shrugged off her coat, overcome with the heat in the reception area of the lodge.

Nora smiled. "Shoveling kind of gets you heated up, doesn't it?"

"I'll say."

"How did you get over here anyway? The snow is so deep. The main road isn't plowed yet, is it?"

And there it was. The question she didn't want to answer. She squirmed then looked at Nora. "I... uh... I stayed the night at Jason's. His truck wouldn't start, and it was such a whiteout with the storm."

"Smart choice." Nora nodded and headed to the kitchen.

Bree stood there for a moment, stunned. *Smart choice?* She shook her head and followed Nora to the kitchen.

JASON SAID BARELY a word as he drove her back to her cabin. Thoughts raced through her mind. He regretted last night. It had to be that. It was impossible to ignore the distance he was putting between them.

Like she'd always heard... don't mix

friendship and romance because you might just end up losing a good friend.

He pulled up in front of the cabin and she opened the door. "Thanks for the ride."

"No problem."

She slipped out of the truck and turned to look at him. The look on his face was so obvious, she knew him that well. Regret clouded his eyes. His jaw was set in a firm look of determination.

"Jason—"

"I'd better go. Mom needs me at the lodge. I've got a lot more work to do."

She nodded and closed the truck door before watching him drive away.

They had connected last night, and he'd awoken unexpected feelings inside of her. Thawed her. He was a great kisser, and she'd enjoyed every minute of last night, but nothing was worth losing him as a friend.

She just hoped she hadn't already.

Life got complicated sometimes...

"Hey, Mom." Cody stood in the doorway. "I shoveled the drive. It was kind of fun. Never shoveled snow before."

She smiled and walked to the cabin. "I bet if you lived here all the time you'd get tired of it."

"Maybe." He grinned.

She followed him inside. Cece stood in front of the glass front cabinet of their mother's, boxes and newspaper at her feet.

"Do you want any of this? I kind of hate to give it away." Cece turned to her.

"Mom did have quite the collection of teacups and stemware and plates, didn't she?"

"It's all such a mismatch, but somehow she always made it all look like it worked together when she used them." Cece picked up a wine glass with flowers etched into it.

She shrugged off her coat and went to join her sister. "And this was one of my favorite teacups of hers. Love the tiny purple flowers." She traced her finger over the fine china.

"I was going to pack this all up to donate... but I think I want to keep some of it. I don't have a need for it, so it seems foolish, but I want to keep some of it."

"I do, too. Let's each pack up a box for ourselves, then we'll finish up boxing the rest for donating."

They cleared the cabinet and ended up sitting on the floor, wrapping up the last of the stemware and putting it in the last box.

Cece paused in wrapping a sheet of bubble

wrap around a glass and glanced over at Cody sitting at the table. "So... you stayed with Jason last night?" She kept her voice low.

"I stayed at his cabin. Not *with* him."

"Mm-hmm..." Cece carefully wrapped the glass and set it in the box. "And that's all?"

"That's all."

"You're lying." Cece grinned.

"What?"

"You have those two spots of pink on your cheeks and you keep shoving that lock of hair behind your ear. It's your tell, sis. It means you're hedging the truth."

"I..." She glanced over at Cody and whispered. "Okay, well he might have kissed me last night."

"I told you he liked you." A self-satisfied look crossed her face.

"But then today he totally ignored me. Totally. He's... well, I can tell he regrets it. And maybe now we've messed up our friendship."

"Or maybe you just need to give it some time." Cece wrapped another glass and handed it to Bree to put in the box.

"We don't really have time, though. I'm leaving as soon as we get the house ready. And we're getting close."

And suddenly she didn't want to be finished with the house repairs and the packing. She didn't want to think of the cabin not being theirs any longer. Her heart clenched in her chest, and a feeling of loss washed over her.

"Cece... I..." She sprung to her feet. "Let's take a break."

"You don't have to say that twice." Cece crawled up from the floor and stretched. She glanced at her watch. "Oh, Petey called. He's coming for the weekend. His Friday class was cancelled, so he's driving over this evening. That's okay with you, isn't it?"

"Of course." Bree headed to the kitchen with Cece right behind her. "Besides, he's the best painter of all of us."

"Years of experience. I swear he wanted his room a different color every year. I finally said he had to do it himself. So he did. And he'd paint my room, the kitchen, any room I wanted. And he's pretty handy at repairs, too. Dad taught him all of that."

A pang shivered through Bree. Her father could have shown Cody how to do all that too. And shown him all about photography, another passion of his. But because of her stubbornness, none of that had happened.

She drew a glass of water, and stood looking out the window as she sipped the cool liquid. After they sold the cabin, she'd never stand here at this sink and look out the window at the pine trees and the birds flying overhead. She'd never sit out by the lake and watch the sunset. She might never even return to Sweet River Falls.

Cody came into the cabin and stood beside her. "It's a great view, isn't it?"

"It really is."

"I'm glad I got to come and see the cabin and Sweet River Falls. You know, before you sell it."

"It's harder than I thought to sell this place, but we really can't keep it. Can't afford to."

"That's a shame. I wish..." His voice trailed off.

"You wish, what?" She turned to look directly at him.

"I wish I'd come here as a kid. Like Petey. I wish I'd known my grandparents better. Pete was telling me some great stories about going out fishing with Granddad."

"Cody, I'm sorry, too. I'm sorry I pulled away from my family. I'm sorry you didn't get to experience all of that growing up. It's totally on me. My fault. I just closed off from everyone when it happened."

"Kind of like how you closed off from me when Dad left you?"

Her jaw dropped, and she set her glass carefully on the counter before she had a chance to drop it. "I—" She reached out and touched his face. "I didn't do that, did I?"

"You did. I felt like you pulled away and kind of like I lost both of you when Dad moved out."

"Oh, Cody, I'm so sorry."

"I know, Mom. I know it was hard on you. It was hard on me, too. I finally decided to go live with Dad and give you your space. I was afraid I was a constant reminder of Dad. I guess that's how you felt about Petey, too, huh? A constant reminder of Peter?"

She sagged against the counter. "Oh, I'm just so sorry you felt that way. I didn't mean to pull away." But she had. She could see that clearly now that he'd pointed it out. Once again she'd made it about herself, what Brian leaving her had done to *her*. Her pain. She really wasn't liking seeing this side of herself.

"Cody, I don't know how I can ever make it up to you. I can't. But I am sorry. I hope now we can... I don't know... find a way to get back to what we had?"

"It's cool, Mom. I'm fine. I'm just... tired of living with Dad and feeling like I'm an imposition."

"You are always welcome to live with me. Always."

He looked at her, and she wasn't sure if she saw gratefulness or skepticism. "Maybe we'll talk about it later, okay?"

"That would be fine. Whenever you want to talk." She took a step closer to him and wrapped him in a hug. "I love you so much."

"Love you too, Mom." He settled down at the table to work on his photos again.

She turned to look out the window. She had so dreaded coming to the cabin. Being here again. But surprisingly, coming back to this cabin had made such a difference in her life, as if it wanted to help her heal.

A knock at the door broke through her thoughts and she went to answer it.

"Hey." Jason stood in the doorway.

"Hi, come on in." She stood aside for him to enter.

"Hey, Jason." Cece came to stand beside

her, then turned and said, "I'll be in the kitchen if you need me."

"I do need you," Jason said.

Cece stopped."What?"

"I have such a big favor to ask you two."

"What's that?" Bree eyed him.

"We have a wedding at the lodge this weekend. Saturday. And the bride just called. The caterer she hired had a fire and cancelled on her. She asked if Mom could help out with the food as best she could." He turned to Bree. "Please, can you help her? Can you pull something together by Saturday night?"

Bree shook her head. "That doesn't give us much time."

"So you'll do it?" Jason reached out and took her hand. "Please?"

"Yes, I'll do it." She turned to Cece. "You want to help?"

"Of course I will."

"Tell your mother I'll be glad to help. Let me get some thoughts together on what we could do so last minute and give me the bride's phone number."

"The bride is at the lodge already."

"All right. I'll come and talk to her now."

"I really appreciate this. I know Mom said

she would do what she can, but she's already too busy with everything."

Bree picked up her coat and tugged on her boots. "Let's go. We'll make plans with the bride, then I'll need to go shopping first thing in the morning."

"I'll take you."

"Fine. Let's go."

She climbed into his truck and they said not a word about last night. But somehow a bit of their prior friendship seeped through. Banding together to help out at the lodge. It's what they'd always done.

JASON LOOKED up and saw Beth coming into the lodge with his nephews, Trevor and Connor, trailing behind her. "Hey, sis."

"I called Mom and she said we have kind of an emergency here this weekend. I came to see what I can do to help."

Jason motioned over to where Bree was sitting at a table with the bride. "We've got part of it covered. Bree's going to cater the wedding."

"Bree? I heard she was here in town fixing

up her parents' cabin. She's going to sell it, huh?"

"Mom, we're going to go find Grams," Trevor interrupted.

"She's in the kitchen." Jason nodded toward the kitchen door and the boys headed that direction.

"Well, that's handy to have her in town to help."

"It is."

"I heard her parents died in a car accident. Just like Sophie's did. Man, that is just so tough. No warning. Both of them."

"Yes, I'm sure it's a terrible blow." Jason couldn't imagine. It had been hard enough losing their dad, but they'd known it was coming and could say their goodbyes. He couldn't imagine the shock of losing both parents, suddenly, at once.

"Well, it's lucky for Mom that she's in town to help. I hear she has her own catering business now."

"No secrets in this town."

Bree came over to them. "Beth, hi."

"Hi yourself. You're looking good. I don't think I've seen you in forever."

"No... uh... I haven't been around." She

turned to Jason. "I think I have a game plan for the wedding. The bride was pretty agreeable with everything. She was just grateful I could step in and help. I just need to talk to Nora for a minute."

"She's in the kitchen. If you see two boys in there, chase them back out to me so you two can talk."

"Okay, I will."

Jason didn't miss that Bree's eyes were shining. She seemed excited to have this challenge. He watched her hurry over to the kitchen.

"Ah, so you still have a thing for her." Beth tilted her head.

"What?"

"A thing. You like her. You always did. I never knew why you didn't ask her out. Then Peter..."

"Yes, then Peter."

"So, ask her out now."

"It's not that easy." Jason frowned.

"Because you're always afraid to commit? Because you're afraid people will leave you?"

Ouch.

"That's life, Jason. It is. But if you always

run before you give it a chance... well, you'll die a lonely, bitter old man."

"I'm not bitter. Or old."

"Jason, I love you, but sometimes you think things to death and you take too long to make up your mind."

"She lives in Austin."

"One word. Airplane."

His sister never did cut him any slack. He looked over at the kitchen door where Bree had disappeared. Maybe Beth was right. Maybe he *should* give it a chance.

But she was leaving. Leaving soon. They didn't really have enough time to even see where this was heading. Not that this was really anything yet. All he'd done was kiss her.

Kiss her many times.

And enjoyed it.

But mostly, he loved spending time with her. Talking to her, just being with her. He'd missed her *friendship*.

"Buck up, cowboy. Sometimes life gives us tough decisions to make." Beth walked away and disappeared into the kitchen.

Disappeared. The story of his life.

Maybe he should do something about that...

CHAPTER 19

Bright and early the next morning, Jason took Bree to the market in town to get her supplies. The bride had agreed to appetizers and finger foods. But she had her heart set on a wedding cake, and Bree was going to do anything she could to make that happen for her. She'd made a few wedding cakes but usually passed that job onto a baker she used frequently in Austin. Her own weren't works of art, but they were passable, and they were delicious.

They walked up and down the aisles, and she made a few substitutions based upon what the market had available.

She paused when a woman she didn't know walked up to them.

"Jason, really? I heard the caterer cancelled

for the wedding that was supposed to happen at the lodge this weekend."

Jason stiffened beside her. "The wedding *is* happening, Gloria."

"Surely Nora doesn't think she can actually *cater* a wedding. Her food is just so... plain."

"Her cooking is delicious." She didn't know who this woman was, but she took an instant dislike to her.

"Well, I guess you could call it homey. Though, a bride who would want a wedding at a *rustic* place like the lodge... Well, maybe homey is okay with her."

"Bree's a caterer from Austin." Justin nodded his head toward her. "A great one. She's helping out with the wedding."

Gloria looked her over and gave her a definite I-don't-think-so look.

"I've catered dozens of weddings and even more events. This isn't a problem." Though she was a bit annoyed that she had to defend herself.

"I guess when a real caterer cancels on you, you have to take whatever handouts you get."

"Gloria, we're busy." Jason's words came out as part threat, part dismissal.

"Well, good luck with your little attempt at a

wedding reception. Hope it all works out."
There was not a bit of sincerity in her words.

Jason grabbed her elbow, and she let him
steer them toward the checkout.

"Wow... is she... like real?"

"There's a long-standing feud between
Gloria and Mom. Don't know how it started. It's
pretty much one-sided. Gloria trash talks Mom
and the lodge. Mom ignores her."

"That's probably a good idea. She's
incredibly rude."

"And clueless." He steered the cart.
"And, Bree?"

"What?"

"I'm sure you'll do a great job catering this
wedding and I really appreciate you helping
Mom out like this."

"It's no problem, really. Glad I could help. It
kind of breaks my heart to think of a bride
without any food at her wedding reception."
She smiled.

They paid for the items they'd collected—
two carts full of groceries—and headed out to
the truck.

When they got to the lodge, Jason unloaded
the truck and she stood in the kitchen sorting
out their purchases. Nora and Judy assured her

they'd give her as much kitchen space as possible to work in while they took care of the lodge visitors.

Nora finally left to go work the front desk as people coming to the wedding began to arrive and Cece showed up to help. "I got the boys all set on finishing the painting at the cabin. Thought I'd come help you. I'm not a cook like you or Mom, but I can follow directions like the best of them."

"Thanks, I can use more help." Bree gave her detailed instructions on how to make one of the appetizers. They talked and baked, and Bree couldn't help but think about how it was almost like old times when they'd help their mother in the kitchen. Making pies. Making some of Mom's fancy appetizers. Bree still used some of her mother's recipes in her catering business.

She could almost—*almost*—believe that she and Cece hadn't drifted apart for all those years.

She looked up to see Jason standing in the doorway and smiling at them.

"Did you come to help?" He seemed less standoffish now. More relaxed. Good. She didn't have time to think about anything but catering the wedding tomorrow.

"I got the rest of the pathways cleared and

was going to help Mom with the check-in, but she said I should come help you instead."

"You sure she doesn't need you?"

"No, she called in some more workers for this weekend. We're good. So, put me to work."

"Do you cook? Bake?"

"I can open a can of chili and heat it up with the best of them. And I can grill steak. And I make great coffee."

Cece laughed. "Those are really going to help, I bet. Maybe you can just take directions like I'm doing."

"Good plan." He walked over to the sink and scrubbed his hands. "Okay, what do you want me to do?"

"I'm getting ready to put the cake together. You want to help with that?"

"I do. I think. I mean, what if I screw it up?"

"Then we'll have to bake more cake, so let's try and do it right the first time."

Jason stayed and helped Bree for the rest of the afternoon and evening, pausing only to help out in the dining room for a bit during the dinner rush. He was impressed by her creativity and efficiency as she made the food for the wedding.

His mother and Judy finally left, promising to be back early in the morning to help with whatever they could.

"I'm almost finished with what I can get done tonight." Bree glanced at her watch. "Cece, why don't you head back to the cabin and check on the boys."

"I'm not going to argue with you. I'm exhausted. But I plan on helping you again tomorrow."

"I thought I'd ask the boys if they'd come help serve at the wedding."

"I bet they would. Wonder if Petey has anything decent to wear..."

"I thought I'd send them to town to buy just white shirts, or blue shirts, or something like that and khakis. That's going to have to do." Bree jotted a note.

"You've thought of everything," Jason said appreciatively.

"I'm sure I'm forgetting something, but it was all so last minute." Bree sank onto a stool by the counter.

"I'm sure it will all be fine. The cake turned out great."

"It did, didn't it? I'm kind of proud of it."

"Well, if you're sure you don't need me, I'm outta here." Cece picked up her coat. "I'll see you later back at the cabin?"

Jason didn't miss that it was a question, not a statement.

"Of course. I'll be home soon."

Suddenly they were alone in the big kitchen. An awkward silence settled over them.

"Breester—"

"Jason—"

He laughed. "You go first."

She looked up at him, a streak of flour on her flushed cheeks. "I know you were... I mean, you were, I don't know—*something*—yesterday."

"Bree, I—"

"No, let me finish." She held up a hand. "I don't want anything to jeopardize our friendship. I know you regret what happened the other night."

"No, I—"

She held up her hand again. "We're good as friends. We are. I'd forgotten how much I enjoy being with you, talking with you. Let's not screw that up now that we've found it again, okay?"

He could see the determination in her eyes. He'd really messed this one up. First taking so long to kiss her, then deciding it was wrong. And now that Beth—in her strident, sensible sister way—had convinced him to take another chance, it was too late.

That also was the story of his life. Too late.

His heart tightened. "If that's really what you want, Bree."

"It is."

She stood and moved over to the counter to finish her work.

He stood and battled his feelings. He could argue with her. Say they should at least try. But he knew how she was when she'd made up her mind. And he could clearly see her mind was made up on this.

Well, at least he had his friend back. Maybe they could still remain friends even with the distance between them.

But he didn't really hold out a lot of hope for that...

CHAPTER 20

The wedding turned out better than Bree had imagined. The bride decided to move the wedding inside since another storm was brewing. The reception area of the lodge, with the big fireplace, was the perfect backdrop. Jason set up chairs for the attendees, and everything turned out beautifully.

The bride and her family were so grateful that she'd stepped in to cater the reception. The boys had helped serve drinks and appetizers. It couldn't have turned out better if she'd planned it all for months.

She finished up cleaning up the dishes and put some leftover appetizers in the fridge. Nora came up beside her with another tray of glasses she'd gathered.

"You did such a wonderful job. I'm so glad the bride was able to have the wedding she wanted."

"I'm glad I was here to help."

Nora set the tray on the counter. "You know, the nearest good caterer to Sweet River Falls is in Denver. It's a shame, really. We have weddings here, and the Pine Valley B&B has small ones in the garden behind their building. I keep thinking someone will start up a wedding planning business here in town. More people are choosing the area for a destination wedding."

"Well, it sure is a beautiful place to get married. All those windows in the lodge looking over the lake. The sunset was spectacular tonight. I saw that her photographer took her outside with the groom and got some wonderful photos. Cody was watching them the whole time."

"Jason said Cody's got a real thing for photography and Hunt's been teaching him."

"He has." She glanced around the kitchen to make sure all the food was put away, then turned back to Nora. "So are Beth and Mac going to get married here, I assume?"

"They are. As soon as they pick a date. She

actually asked me if you'd be willing to cater it. Do you think you could come back and do that?"

"Oh... I don't know. I... suppose so." Bree's mind whirled. It would give her a chance to come back to Sweet River Falls. She'd like that, wouldn't she? Though, the cabin might be sold by then, so she'd have to find a place to stay.

"Have her get with me on the date, and I'll check." That gave her an out if she changed her mind, right? It just might be too hard to come back here after the cabin was sold, too painful.

BREE AWOKE the next morning to the sound of laughter drifting through the cabin. She sat up and stretched. Cody's laugh rang out again and she smiled. It was wonderful to have the sounds of family laughter in the cabin again.

She climbed out of bed, grabbed her robe, and headed to the kitchen for some much-needed coffee.

"Hey, Mom." Cody sat at the table with his laptop and camera in front of him.

Cece came walking out of the kitchen and

handed her a mug of coffee. "Thought you might need this. Long day yesterday."

"It was, but it turned out great, don't you think? And boys, I can't thank you enough for helping serve."

"Nora paid us both." Petey walked out of the kitchen. "She said she usually had enough staff to help, but they were shorthanded a bit. She also offered me a job to help out at the lodge when they have busy weekends."

"Really?"

"Yep, and I can stay in the summer staff barracks. She also offered me a summer job. She's a cool lady."

"Hey, can we talk?" Cody walked over to her.

"Of course."

He nodded to the couch on the far side of the great room and she followed him over.

"So, I've made some decisions and hope you're going to be okay with them."

She held her breath. The last big decision he'd made was to go live with his Dad.

"So, I'm thinking about going to Mountain Grove College. I think I'll get in. My test scores are great, and I've kept up a good GPA. If it works out, Petey and I talked about sharing an apartment. I'm going to go visit the school tomorrow when he goes back. I thought I'd spend the night there tomorrow, and he said he could bring me back to the cabin on Tuesday."

She sat back on the couch and tried not to look stunned.

"Also, Nora offered me a job this summer, too, along with Pete. Did you know he likes to be called Pete, not Petey? Anyway, we said yes to Nora. We're going to work at the lodge." He looked at her. "I hope all this is okay with you."

"I—" She swallowed."It's fine with me. I think you'll love working at the lodge this summer."

Cody grinned. "I hoped you'd say it was okay."

She was just glad he was even asking her opinion anymore.

"You'll come up and visit this summer, won't you?" He started to stand.

"I... well, I hadn't really thought about it."

"You should." Cody stood and headed for the table, pulling out his phone. "I'm going to text Hunt, too. Maybe I can go out on more photo shoots with him this summer."

Cece came over and sat beside her. "So, you heard the great plan, huh? You okay with that?"

"I'm strangely very okay with it. I mean, he'll still be far away from me, but... I'm glad he and Petey—*Pete*—have become friends."

"Ah, you heard about the name change. He says he's too old to be called Petey. It's going to take a bit to remember that. Apparently all his friends at college call him Pete."

"They grow up, don't they?" Bree glanced over to where the two boys were talking at the table and looking at Cody's photos on his laptop.

"Too quickly," Cece agreed.

"Well, they'll love working at the lodge. It's hard work, but it's fun being with all the kids working there for the summer."

"You're okay with Mountain Grove College?"

"Definitely. It's a great school."

"I'll just be in Denver if they need anything. And they can come to my house on the weekends if they just want to get away for a few days." Cece leaned forward. "So, you're really okay?"

"I really am." She was. A sense of peace settled over her at the idea of Cody being in Sweet River Falls. Maybe he could have some magical summers like she'd had when she was young.

The only thing she was sorry about was she'd still be so far away from him. She'd secretly harbored the hope he might come back to Texas for college. But this was second best. She tried to convince herself that all kids eventually left home and went to college or went out on their own. But she still ached deep inside for the time she'd missed with him.

CHAPTER 21

Bree stood at the cabin door and waved as the boys left early the next morning to get back to Mountain Grove for Pete's classes. Cody had chattered away this morning about seeing the campus, how great it was going to be, and every tiny detail that Pete had told him about going to school there.

She hadn't seen him this excited about something since... well, since Hunt had asked him on the photo shoot. Cody had come out of his normal quiet shell he'd had around her the last few years, and she relished every moment. It was going to be so hard to head back to Austin and not see him every day.

She closed the door, pushing it shut. *Really* needed to fix that before showing the cabin.

"Here's another cup of coffee." Cece headed over with a steaming mug in her hand. "I didn't think we were going to get them out the door in time."

Bree perched on the edge of the couch and took a sip of the coffee. "We still have so much to do here."

"We do. There's a lot of years to pack up and a lot of sprucing up to do. At least the boys finished the painting. It does look a lot better."

"I... I'm going to miss this place. Coming back here after all this time... I have so many regrets. I wish..." It didn't help to make wishes. What happened, happened.

"So, I was thinking." A serious look crossed Cece's face. "Why don't we try and keep the cabin?"

"We've been over this. None of us have enough money to keep it."

"I have some savings I could contribute."

Bree eyed her sister."You do?"

"And I was thinking something else." Cece paused and looked directly at her. "What's keeping you in Austin?"

"You mean besides my business?"

"Cody's not there anymore, and he's coming to Colorado for college most likely. You could..." Cece took a deep breath. "You could move back here to Sweet River Falls and live at the cabin.

"I can't just drop everything and move here."

"Sure you could. You'd be close to Cody. And Nora said there wasn't a caterer around here in a six-town radius. You could open up your catering company here. I know you'd have lots of business."

"I've worked so hard to build up things in Austin." Bree frowned. "But Jolene has made a few comments about maybe going out on her own... I wonder if she'd want to buy my business."

"Perfect idea."

"If I sold my house in Austin, I'd have money for the taxes, insurance, and upkeep here, but I don't have enough money to buy out both you and Abby. Have you checked the market value of this cabin?"

"You don't have to buy me out. Just let me come stay here sometimes."

"Really?"

"Really. I'd love nothing more than to still have the cabin in the family. We could have holidays here with the boys. It would be wonderful." Cece nodded her head emphatically.

"But that still doesn't solve the Abby problem. I don't have enough to give her a third of the value of the cabin."

"Maybe we could talk her into... I don't know, taking payments or something?" Cece's forehead creased. "Though, I'm not sure why she's so worried about getting her split. She's the only one of the three of us that has it made. She jaunts all around the country. Drives her fancy car. Lives in that condo that has to be worth a bazillion bucks."

"I guess I could try talking to her." The idea of staying in Sweet River Falls was beginning to grow on her. She was tired of the hustle and bustle of Austin. Tired of the endless traffic. Maybe she could make a go of a catering business here.

And since she and Jason had decided to just remain friends, she'd have a good friend... if she really did move here.

She looked around the cabin and started laughing.

"What's so funny?"

"Just look at all the work we've done boxing everything up." She flung her hand wide.

Cece burst out laughing. "Well, if we can work this out, I'll help you unpack."

BREE WALKED into the kitchen at the lodge and found Nora busy making loaves of bread.

"Bree, hi. You looking for Jason? He ran into town."

"No, I was looking for you." She walked over and plopped down on a stool by the counter.

"You found me. What can I do for you?" Nora pounded on the bread dough, working it and folding it over and over.

"I want to run something past you."

"Shoot."

"Well, I was talking to Cece, and we decided we're going to try and keep the cabin."

Nora broke into a wide grin. "Well, that's good news. I hated to think of you girls giving it up."

"Well, I still have to make some things happen first." Like convince Abby to let her pay her off over time, but she didn't want to share that with Nora. "Anyway, I'm actually thinking of moving here. Back to Sweet River Falls."

"Why that would be wonderful. We'd love having you around."

"I was... well, I was thinking of starting up a catering business here in town. I could cater events here and in Mountain Grove and maybe even get into some of the wedding planning business."

"I'd sure turn wedding planning for the weddings here over to you. You want the job?"

Bree laughed. "Well, I do. Let me see if I can make this happen."

"Make what happen?" Jason walked into the kitchen and swiped a cookie from the tray of them beside Nora.

Nora tilted her head toward Jason. "Go ahead, you tell him."

"I'm trying to make things work out so we can keep the cabin."

"That's great news." A wide smile spread across his face.

"Tell him the other part." Nora nodded.

"Oh, that." She grinned. "And if things work out, I think I'm moving to Sweet River Falls."

Jason's eyebrows rose and he sucked in a quick breath."Really?"

"If I can work things out with Abby."

"That's great news, Bree. Great." His smile was so broad that the faint lines at the sides of his eyes deepened.

It would be nice to have a good friend here. She'd missed Jason and their easy camaraderie. Well, at least until they'd messed it up with a kiss. They could make their way back to friendship, she was sure they could.

Pretty sure...

Her phone vibrated in her pocket and she dug it out. A text from Abby. "Well, that's strange."

"What?" Jason asked.

"Abby texted and said she's flying to Denver and is coming to the cabin. She'll be here tonight. Wonder what that's about." She shrugged. "But at least I'll get a chance to talk to her."

CHAPTER 22

That evening after finishing up his work at the lodge, Jason stood in front of the mirror in his bathroom. He'd showered, put on a clean shirt, combed his hair. As an afterthought, he slapped on some aftershave. He was going to head over to Bree's cabin and talk to her.

No more overthinking.

No more waiting.

The universe had given him a second chance, and he wasn't going to blow it this time. He grabbed his jacket and headed out.

He drove over to the cabin, reciting different words, different ways to say what he wanted to say to her. When he pulled his truck into the drive at Bree's cabin, he turned off the engine and sat for a moment, still trying to think of the right words to say to her. He frowned when he saw the rental car in the driveway. That meant Abby was already here.

He'd just ask Bree if she'd go for a drive with him. Or maybe walk up to the gazebo. They'd have some privacy there. He rubbed his hands on his jeans. It was going to be okay. It was.

He opened the door, hopped out, and walked to the door of the cabin with determined strides.

BREE AND CECE sat on the couch facing Abby, perched on the chair across from them. "So, I —*we*—have decided we want to try and keep the cabin in the family," Bree started, still uncertain why Abby had returned.

Abby raised an eyebrow. "You have?"

"We just can't let it go. So we've come up with a plan," Cece added.

"What's that?"

"Well, if you'll let me pay off your portion over time, I think we can make it work."

"Over how long?"

"Honestly, I'm not sure. I promise you'll get your share, but it will take me a while. You see, I've decided to move to Sweet River Falls."

"What?"

"I'm going to start up a catering business here in town. And Nora has asked me to coordinate the weddings at the lodge. I'll have enough money after I sell my house and business in Austin to pay you some and have enough for taxes and upkeep of the cabin. Then, as my business grows, I'll be able to pay you more."

"That doesn't work for me." Abby shook her head emphatically.

"Why not? What do you need with more money? You're already doing better than either Bree or me." Cece glared at Abby.

A knock at the door interrupted their conversation. Bree got up, annoyed at the disruption. She opened the door to see Jason standing there looking... she'd swear he looked nervous.

"Bree, I need to talk to you."

"Now's not a good time."

Abby called from across the room."Oh, for sure. Invite Jason in. Then the three of you can gang up on me."

Jason stood there uncertainly. She grabbed his hand and pulled him in. "We're kind of in the middle of a discussion on the cabin."

"Yes, Cece and Bree are telling me how we're going to keep the cabin, but I'm not going to get my share of it." Abby stood.

"Don't be like that." Cece slapped her hand on her leg.

"Like what? Like the odd man out? Like the outsider?" Abby's eyes flashed. "I told you I need that money. I need it. I can't wait for some supposed payoff in the future."

"I have a little bit saved. I could help with giving you your share," Cece offered.

"Would it be a third of the value of the cabin? Have you researched market value here? This cabin is a sweet deal now if we sell."

"Don't you have any desire to keep the cabin in the family?" Cece's eyes blazed in anger.

"Not really. I just need my share."

Bree sank down on the couch. "Well, that's that then. I can't come up with that kind of cash. I guess we'll have to sell."

"That's what we planned anyway." Abby stood firm.

"Abby, you can be so self-centered at times." Cece got up and headed for the bedroom.

"Of course, this is all my fault. I'm the one being selfish. It's always my fault." Abby grabbed her coat. "I'm going into town. I'll be back later." She slammed out the door.

JASON SAT DOWN NEXT to Bree. "I'm sorry. I know you really wanted to keep the cabin."

"It just wasn't mean to be." She slowly swept her view around the cabin. "I thought that maybe Abby would go for me paying her off over time."

For once Jason was sorry that he'd invested every penny he'd saved back into the lodge. He'd give anything to be able to help out Bree financially now. Not that she'd take his money.

He'd picked a fine time to decide to come talk to Bree about their future. If they had one.

"So, are you still planning on staying if you sell the cabin?"

Bree frowned. "I don't know. I do have the business back in Austin."

"I thought you wanted to be near Cody."

"I did. I do. I just... it's all getting complicated. I think I'll just get the cabin ready to sell and head back to Austin and think things over. Maybe this is some sign that I made the wrong decision to move to Sweet River Falls."

Disappointment flooded through Jason. Should he talk to her now? Tell her how he felt?

How did he feel?

What he wanted was time together to figure it out.

He could hear the universe laughing at him.

CHAPTER 23

B ree got up the next morning to find Abby gone without a word, and a scribbled note from Cece that she'd gone into town. She went to make coffee and found they didn't have any. That was not going to work for her this morning.

She grabbed her keys from the key drawer, once again noticing the keychain with her parents' keys on it. Her heart crumbled. They were gone. The cabin would soon be gone. She'd tried, she had. It was like the world was conspiring against her.

She headed for Bookish Cafe. Annie greeted her when she entered. "Good morning. I guess the Stuart girls are all on the same wavelength this morning."

"What?"

"Abby was in early this morning, but left. Then Cece was in just a while ago."

Bree gave her a wry smile. "We're out of coffee at the cabin."

Annie handed her a cup of coffee. "Here you go. On the house."

"Is Cece still here?" Bree looked around and glanced toward the stairs leading up to the loft area.

"No, she took hers outside. Said she was going to walk along the river. It's nice out today, isn't it?"

Bree almost laughed at the "nice out" comment. The sun was shining, and the wind had died down, but it was still cold. This sure wasn't what they'd consider a nice day in Austin. Guess it was all relative.

"I think I'll do the same." She headed out into the sunshine and wandered along the pathway by the river. The gurgle of the stream and the sunlight glinting off the water enchanted her. She did so love this town. She came to the end of the path where it opened to a large brick courtyard and froze.

There in the middle of the courtyard was Cece.

And Jason.

Jason was holding Cece in his arms. He pushed a lock of hair away from her face and swept a finger across her cheek.

Bree closed her eyes as the familiar feeling of anger and betrayal swept over her. Her breath came in an empty gasp, and her pulse slowed as if the world was revolving in slow motion. She fought the feeling, opened her eyes, and stalked over to them.

"Well, I guess it all worked out what with not being able to keep the cabin." Her words were brittle and cold.

"What?" Jason dropped his arms from around Cece and turned and smiled at her.

Smiled at her.

"So I know we said that we'd just be friends. That's probably a great idea, right?"

"What do you mean?" Jason frowned.

"Well, it was bad enough that Cece slept with my boyfriend, but now that you and her are a thing, I'm leaving." She whirled around.

"No, wait..."

"No, I'm serious. Leave me alone. Just leave me alone."

Bree wasn't giving either of them time to explain.

She was done with her sister. Done with Jason. Done with Sweet River Falls.

"I'VE GOT to go after her." Jason started to follow Bree.

Cece put her hand on his arm. "I think she needs a minute. She's so angry now. She said to leave her alone. Maybe give her time to cool off."

"I don't know..." He eyed Cece. "Are you okay?"

"No." Cece shook her head. "Everything is even more messed up now." She swiped a tear from her cheek. "Thank you for listening to me. I was so upset."

"It wasn't like I was going to just leave you here crying."

"Our timing was kind of lousy, though, wasn't it? Bree thinks that we're... a thing."

"I'll go talk to her. Sort it out."

"She might not believe you."

"She either trusts me or not. If she doesn't, then... well, we don't have anything to base a relationship on anyway."

"You want a relationship with her, don't you?"

"More than anything."

"I thought that we'd worked things out and Bree would be moving back close again. Then Abby blew that up. And now this. Maybe none of this was meant to be." Cece let out a long sigh.

Jason squared his shoulders. "Maybe all of this *is* meant to be. Maybe we're just giving up too quickly."

Cece looked at him and nodded. "You're right. Let's go find her."

CHAPTER 24

Abby was actually in the cabin packing when Bree returned. Great. Just what she needed. Abby looked up from where she was packing up their mother's vases."Mom had a ton of these, didn't she?" Abby said the words as if it was the most normal thing to say. Like she hadn't just blown up Bree's plan to keep the cabin. As if Bree hadn't just found Cece in Jason's arms.

"She did." That was all Bree could get out. She headed to the bedroom to get away. Away from Abby. Away from Cece. Away from everything. She looked around wildly, wondering how long it would take to finish up the cabin.

What if she just went back to Austin and left her sisters to finish up? That would serve them right. She'd done more than her share.

She swung her suitcase from the closet and started throwing her clothes in it. Then she collapsed on the bed. But Cody was still here. She couldn't bear to leave Cody. She flung herself backward and threw her hands over her head.

"Bree?" Jason's voice came from the open doorway.

Nope, not going to happen. "Go away."

"No, we're going to talk to you and you're going to listen." Cece walked into the room, her voice firmer than Bree had ever heard it.

Cece reached out and pulled on Bree's hands, making her sit up on the bed. "Now, you need to listen to us."

Bree closed her eyes, willing them to disappear.

"Jason found me crying out on the walkway by the river. I was upset that you were leaving. We were so close to making things work out."

"I was just trying to comfort her. I couldn't just leave her there crying." She heard Jason step into the room and opened her eyes.

"I know you don't have any reason to trust me. I know that. But, please, don't let this mess things up," Cece pleaded.

Jason looked right into her eyes. "Nothing happened except I was trying to comfort a friend. You either believe me or you don't." His eyes flashed with defiance.

She looked deep into his eyes and knew the truth. She did believe him. She did trust him. He'd promised he'd never lie, never keep anything from her ever again.

She stood and a blush of embarrassment swept through her. "I'm sorry. I'm sorry to both of you. I shouldn't have jumped to conclusions. I'm... sorry."

A look of relief crept over Cece's face.

Jason held out a hand and pulled her into his strong arms, wrapping them securely around her.

Cece smiled and slipped out of the room.

They stood there silently for a long time. His heartbeat pounding against her cheek pressed against him. His hand stroking her back. She could almost believe that things were okay.

Almost.

"BREE, come sit on the bed. I want to talk to you." They finally pulled apart.

They sat side by side on her bed amidst her clothes strewn around them.

He sucked in a deep breath and took her hands in his. "I want you to stay. I want us to be together. Figure out what we have." He paused and squeezed her hands. "No, that's not the truth."

She watched him closely.

"I know what we have, I've just been afraid to admit it." He could barely hear his words through the pounding of his pulse. "I love you, Bree. I think I've loved you since we were kids. Since I first met you. I'm not letting this chance get away from us. Not this time."

"You what? Can you say that again?"

He could barely hear her words.

"I love you, Bree. I want you to stay. Say you'll stay here with me. Move back here."

"But the cabin and... everything."

"We'll find you a place to live. We'll work it out."

She smiled up at him then, tears crowding the corner of her eyes. "I love you, too."

"So you'll stay?"

"So I'll stay."

He leaned down and kissed her then, a long tender kiss on her welcoming lips.

He'd finally gotten his timing right.

CHAPTER 25

Bree and Jason walked into the great room, hand in hand. Her heart was soaring. She barely noticed the stacks of boxes. Her anger toward Abby slipped away, smothered out by her happiness.

The door opened and Pete and Cody entered the cabin, laughing. Cody stopped when he saw her holding Jason's hand. "Well, it's about time." He grinned at her.

She grinned right back at him.

Cece and Abby came out of the kitchen area. "Hi, boys." Cece walked over and hugged Pete.

"I only had an early class today, so I decided to run Cody back here to the cabin." Pete looked over his mother's shoulder. "Aunt Abby, you're back."

"I came to help pack up."

"I thought Mom said Aunt Bree was going to stay in the cabin and we weren't going to sell." Pete glanced at Cody. "Darn it. Mom said not to say anything until your mom had a chance to talk to you."

"Mom, are you staying at the cabin?" Cody looked at her.

"I was trying to work it out. But I can't quite swing the money."

"I'm sorry boys, but I need my portion of the proceeds from the sale." Abby set down a box she was holding. "I have some... debts... I need to pay off."

Bree turned and frowned at Abby. "What kind of debts?"

"I..." Abby blushed. "I have some gambling debts."

"Gambling. I didn't know you gambled." Cece walked over to Abby.

"It appears I'm also horrible with money. I'm just in over my head now."

Bree thought about Abby's fancy, expensive condo and car. She wasn't sure about this whole needing money thing.

Abby's eyes filled with tears. "I'm selling my condo. I already sold my car. I'm moving to a tiny, crummy apartment." She let out a long sigh. "My life is a mess. If I could afford to let you pay me off over time, I would. I just don't have the time, and I'm running out of options."

Bree walked over and put a hand on Abby's arm. "Why didn't you just tell us?"

"I was so ashamed. I'm terrible with money, really I am. I never seem to have anything left over."

Pete walked up to them. "So, Aunt Bree was going to stay at the cabin and pay off Aunt Abby's portion over time? And, Mom, you're okay with keeping the cabin? You don't need the money from the sale?"

"I'm fine with it. I wanted to keep the cabin in the family. It's breaking my heart to think other people will own it. They'll be here with their families. Making their own memories." Cece sighed. "But, it's just what it is."

"What if I bought out Aunt Abby?"

"You?" Cody's eyes widened.

"I have some money from Dad's parents. It was a trust they'd established for Dad... but then he died. It's mine now. What if I own part of the cabin? Would that work?"

"Petey—*Pete*—are you sure you want to spend the trust money on the cabin?" Cece placed her hand on her son's arm.

"I like having the cabin. I like that we've been together here these last few weeks. It would be cool to have Aunt Bree here, too. I have the scholarship for college. I'm doing fine."

"I could pay you back over time." Bree looked at Pete and could only see Peter standing there. Offering her a way to make things work out. In a strange way, it felt like Peter was asking for forgiveness.

"Or I could be part owner of the cabin." Pete shrugged.

Cece threw her arms around him. "I think it's a wonderful idea. A good investment for you, too, the way the prices are rising around here."

Cody grinned. "This is turning out to be one of the best trips ever." He turned to her. "And if you're staying here... would you mind if I moved in with you? I'm kind of tired of being in the way at Dad's... and... I've missed you, Mom."

She gave him a big hug, so glad to have him here where she could wrap her arms around him. "Yes, of course. I'd love that."

"I still think I want to live in the barracks at

the lodge with the other kids this summer. Is that okay?"

"Yes, that's fine." He'd still be here. Near her. She'd see him and have a chance to get close to him again. Her world was settling into place faster than she could ever have imagined.

Jason stepped forward. "Abby, if you'll let me, I could help you sort out your debts. Help you make a budget."

"You should let him. Nora says he's kind of a genius with money." Bree smiled at Jason.

"I accept. I think I need all the help I can get."

"Perfect." Jason walked back to Bree and draped his arm around her shoulders. It felt right and comfortable, and she was just where she needed to be.

"We've got one more complication, though." Jason looked down at her.

"What's that?" Bree frowned.

"Mom said that Beth and Mac need to move their wedding up because Beth insists Sophie has to be here, and Sophie and Chase are leaving for a world tour. So, they're planning on getting married in two weeks. Think you guys can pull it off?"

Bree grinned. "Boys, you going to help serve again?"

"We're in." Pete grinned.

"I can come back and help, too." Cece stood with her arm around Pete.

And just like that, the Stuart girls made peace with their past and their present. Bree looked at her sisters. The sisters who finally had a future together again.

Yes, everything was right in her world.

Everyone started talking and laughing at once, and Jason pulled her aside, standing in front of her with his arms around her waist. "It's good to see you so happy, Breester."

"It feels good to be this happy." Her heart filled with joy and contentment. She'd never felt so happy, like she was right where she belonged.

He gave her a lopsided grin. "I'm hoping to make you even happier."

"I'm not sure that's possible."

"We'll see, Breester. We'll see." He gave her a quick kiss as if making her a promise.

CHAPTER 26

Beth stood in her mother's cabin getting ready for the wedding. She glanced at her watch for the hundredth time. "I'm afraid Sophie isn't going to make it."

"She'll make it if she can. That snow storm has all the flight travel snarled." Nora stood behind Beth, brushing her hair.

"I can't get married without Sophie here. I can't."

"Of course you can. I know that Sophie will be disappointed, but Mac is here. That's the only one that truly matters."

"You're right." Beth sighed. "But I still want her here."

The door to the cabin flew open, and a burst

of cold air and snow blew in. "I'm here." Sophie rushed over and hugged Beth.

"I thought your flight got cancelled."

"About that. We only made it as far as Kansas City. But then Chase found us a flight to Albuquerque. Then we rented a car. Long drive. But I'm here."

Beth hugged her friend. "I'm so glad you made it."

"There's nothing that could have kept me away. Even a silly snow storm. Though we lost our luggage along the way. I had a dress picked out, but now I'll need to run to my apartment and find something."

"You can come just like you are. I don't care."

Sophie kissed her cheek. "You just give me a few minutes. I'll be back with a dress and I'll help you finish getting ready."

Beth looked at her mother after Sophie left. "Now, *now* I feel like it's going to be the perfect wedding."

NORA SAT by Annie's side and watch as Beth

and Mac recited their vows. She couldn't be more pleased with Beth's choice. Mac was a fine man and made her daughter happy. Jason, Trevor, and Connor stood beside Beth and Mac. Along with Sophie... who was crying and swiping at the tears rolling down her cheeks.

"She looks beautiful," Annie whispered.

"She does." Nora looked at her friend sitting next to her husband. Nick had Annie's hand firmly in his.

So much happiness surrounded her today. She didn't know what the future may bring, but right now, in this moment, everything was just perfect.

She turned back to Beth and Mac and listened as they spoke the vows they had written together. Words of love and commitment.

She thought back on her own wedding day when she'd married Jason and Beth's father. She missed the man dearly, every single day since he'd passed away. But today, she felt his presence, looking down on his daughter.

Mac kissed Beth and everyone broke into applause. He took Beth's hand, and the smile on his face told Nora everything she needed to know. Mac and Beth were going to be happy.

Very happy. He was going to protect her and be by her side no matter what life threw at them.

And in the end, a person couldn't ask for much more than that, could they?

CHAPTER 27

Jason stood by her side on the hilltop between her cabin and the lodge. Snow fell gently around them, blanketing the landscape with a delicate white covering. She leaned back against him as they watched the last rays of the sun peek through the storm clouds.

"This gazebo was a great addition to the hill." She sighed in contentment.

"It was, if I do say so myself." His voice was a warm kiss against her cheek.

"You know how I said I wanted to make you even happier?"

"Not possible, Jase. Not possible."

He turned her around to face him and tilted her face up to look at him. "I do want to spend my life making you happy. I love you. And I'm so grateful we got this second chance."

"Me, too." She slipped off her glove and reached up to touch his face.

"So... I was thinking... I was wondering..."

She laughed. "Wondering what?"

He dropped to one knee, and her eyes widened.

"I was hoping that you'd marry me. Will you marry me?" He held out a ring in the palm of his hand.

The world stopped. She drew no breath. Her heart swelled in her chest. "Oh, Jason. Yes. Yes, I'll marry you."

He slid the ring on her finger and she stared down at it. He jumped to his feet, scooped her up, and swung her around. She laughed when he finally set her down and kissed her.

She pulled away and looked at him, his face covered in a wide grin. "Oh, and Jase?"

"What?"

"You were right. You did make me even happier."

A self-satisfied look crossed his face and he winked at her. "Told you." Then he kissed her again.

Thank you for reading my story. I hope you enjoyed it. Sign up for my newsletter to be updated with information on new releases, promotions, give-aways, and newsletter-only surprises. The signup is at my website, kaycorrell.com.

Reviews help other readers find new books. I always appreciate when my readers take time to leave an honest review.

I love to hear from my readers. Feel free to contact me at authorcontact@kaycorrell.com

COMFORT CROSSING ~ THE SERIES

The Shop on Main - Book One

The Memory Box - Book Two

The Christmas Cottage - A Holiday Novella (Book 2.5)

The Letter - Book Three

The Christmas Scarf - A Holiday Novella (Book 3.5)

The Magnolia Cafe - Book Four

The Unexpected Wedding - Book Five

The Wedding in the Grove (crossover short story between the Comfort Crossing and Lighthouse Point series - Josephine and Paul from The Letter.)

LIGHTHOUSE POINT ~ THE SERIES

Wish Upon a Shell - Book One

Wedding on the Beach - Book Two

Love at the Lighthouse - Book Three

Cottage near the Point - Book Four

Return to the Island - Book Five

Bungalow by the Bay - Book Six

SWEET RIVER ~ THE SERIES

A Dream to Believe in - Book One

A Memory to Cherish - Book Two

A Song to Remember - Book Three

A Time to Forgive - Book Four

A Summer of Secrets - Book Five

INDIGO BAY ~ a multi-author series of sweet romance

Sweet Sunrise - Book Three

Sweet Holiday Memories - A short holiday story

Sweet Starlight - Book Nine

ABOUT THE AUTHOR

Kay writes sweet, heartwarming stories that are a cross between women's fiction and contemporary romance. She is known for her charming small towns, quirky townsfolk, and enduring strong friendships between the women in her books.

Kay lives in the Midwest of the U.S. and can often be found out and about with her camera, taking a myriad of photographs which she likes to incorporate into her book covers. When not lost in her writing or photography, she can be found spending time with her ever-supportive husband, knitting, or playing with her puppies —two cavaliers and one naughty but adorable Australian shepherd. Kay and her husband also love to travel. When it comes to vacation time, she is torn between a nice trip to the beach or the mountains—but the mountains only get considered in the summer—she swears she's allergic to snow.

Learn more about Kay and her books at kaycorrell.com

While you're there, sign up for her newsletter to hear about new releases, sales, and giveaways.

WHERE TO FIND ME:
kaycorrell.com
authorcontact@kaycorrell.com

Join my Facebook Reader Group. We have lots of fun and you'll hear about sales and new releases first!
https://www.facebook.com/groups/KayCorrell/

facebook.com/KayCorrellAuthor

instagram.com/kaycorrell

pinterest.com/kaycorrellauthor

amazon.com/author/kaycorrell

bookbub.com/authors/kay-correll

Made in the USA
Las Vegas, NV
18 October 2021

32592615R00152